The Tragedy of Brittany Taylor

ERIC BURNS

iUniverse, Inc.
Bloomington

The Tragedy of Brittany Taylor

iUniverse books may be ordered through booksellers or by contacting:

iUniverse
1663 Liberty Drive
Bloomington, IN 47403
www.iuniverse.com
1-800-Authors (1-800-288-4677)

ISBN: 978-1-4759-5320-6 (sc)
ISBN: 978-1-4759-5321-3 (e)

Library of Congress Control Number: 2012918637

Printed in the United States of America

iUniverse rev. date: 10/29/2012

chapter 1

As Jane pulled into the driveway of her parents' home, she felt a sense of dread. Borrowing money from her parents was the last thing that she wanted to be doing. It was humiliating. It was like admitting that she wasn't good enough, that she hadn't lived up to her parents' expectations.

Of course, borrowing money was not the only way that Jane was showing herself to be inferior in her parents' eyes. When she was twenty, she had gotten pregnant. It's not like she hadn't known about birth control either. She'd always told herself that whenever she planned on having sex, she would make the guy wear a condom.

But not the night that had marked the end of the spring semester of her sophomore year. She'd known that she had aced the exam that would admit her into her college's business program. She'd wanted to be an accountant ever since she was in high school, and now she would be one step closer to making that dream come true.

To celebrate, she'd gone to one of her college's end-of-semester frat parties. She'd never been one to take much interest in Greek life, but a couple of her girlfriends were going and she'd known that there would be plenty of booze there to help take off the edge she'd had that whole week because of finals.

Jane hadn't been naïve about the frat guys' intentions. She'd known that their main focus was to get the girls drunk enough to have sex with them. It wasn't going to happen to her, though. She'd make sure of it.

That's what she'd thought anyway. But after several beers and shots of tequila, the hot guy flirting with her on the couch had only seemed hotter than before. It had been all about that moment for her. Nothing else had seemed to matter. She'd been horny; he'd *definitely* been horny. And in the empty bedroom, with them both lying on the bed touching each other, the fact that the guy didn't have a condom—or said he didn't have one just so he wouldn't have to put one on—had only seemed to be a slight inconvenience not worth any further attention, especially since the guy had promised to pull out when he came.

"Once is all it takes." How many times had Jane heard that sentence before? You smoke crystal meth once, you're hooked for life. You huff paint once, you're in diapers for life. You have unprotected sex once, you get knocked up. And still, having known that having unprotected sex could get her pregnant, Jane had still slept with the guy as though he'd actually pull out before it was too late.

Jane had woken up the next morning feeling like a fool. The guy had still been asleep, thank God. She'd quickly slipped her clothes back on and headed back to her dorm to finish packing her things to go home for the summer.

What had the guy's name been anyway? Matt? Chris? She

hadn't been able to remember. She'd never thought she would have gone so low as to have had a one-night stand like this, especially not with some douche-bag frat guy.

But she'd done it. And now she'd have to live with it.

Six weeks later, she'd thrown up. She'd seen enough movies and taken enough sex-ed classes to know what that meant. She was pregnant.

She'd thought about getting in touch with the guy, but it was the summer and she hadn't even known his name. And even if she had managed to find him some way, who's to say he would have been any help? Chances are he would have just told her she was on her own and gone on with his life as though the sexual encounter he'd had with her hadn't amounted to anything more than sex. And it would have been perfectly okay for him to be like that. Plenty of guys had gotten away with it before. It was just the way the sexist world worked.

She had, however, managed to get in touch with the guy. He had been friends with the frat guy her friend Carla had been dating. Matt was his name, just as she had thought. Anyway, Matt's advice for her had been to get an abortion. He'd wanted no involvement; it would have been too much of an inconvenience to his party life. It was just as Jane had expected. There had been absolutely no use in telling the worthless prick.

Telling her parents had been the worst part. They were infuriated, especially her father. The fact that she hadn't been in a relationship with the baby's father had made it even worse. As far as her parents were concerned, she'd been sleeping around with anyone and everyone; she'd had no respect for herself or her body. She'd become a disgrace to the family.

Things had only become more heated between Jane and

her parents when Jane's plans for the baby collided with her parents' plans. While neither Jane nor her parents supported abortion, their thoughts on what would be done with the baby once he or she was born had been conflicting. While Jane's parents had had high hopes that she would give the baby up for adoption and go back to school the following spring as though nothing had ever happened, Jane had insisted on keeping the baby and raising it herself. She'd known that she wouldn't be able to stand the heartbreak of giving the baby up.

In the end, Jane had been forced to drop out of college in order to pursue a low-paying, full-time job. Her parents had given her a strict upbringing and would not let their daughter get away with bringing a child into the world and raising it while not having a job or the means with which to support the baby.

It may seem that Jane's parents had been unnecessarily cruel and insensitive toward their daughter. On the contrary, her parents had wanted Jane to learn from her mistakes. They had wanted her to become a responsible mother, a mother who would put her child before herself at all times. By refusing to pay Jane's college tuition for the upcoming years, they had left her with no choice but to set aside her own needs and desires for her baby's. And while Jane couldn't help but be a little bitter toward them because of this, she knew she couldn't go as far as to hate them. She was the one who'd messed up, and all they were doing was making her take responsibility for it.

Jane had managed on her own for nearly seven years now. While pregnant with her daughter, Brittany, she had been hired to work full-time at a local supermarket and had managed to save up enough money to get her own place before Brittany was even born. A month and a half after Brittany's birth, Jane had gone right back to work, putting her daughter in daycare aside from the couple days of the week that her parents would watch her. But other than that, Jane had not relied on her parents one bit. No money, nothing.

Until now, of course. Money had always been tight, but now, with prices beginning to rise on groceries, gasoline, and other necessities, Jane saw no option but to turn to her parents.

JANE'S PARENTS WERE EXPECTING THEIR daughter and granddaughter at their doorstep. Jane had asked them for the money over the phone the night before. And now, she had shamefully arrived with her daughter to pick it up.

"Well, hello!" said Jane's mother as she opened the front door.

"Hi, Mom," said Jane as her mother stepped down onto the porch and gave her a hug.

"Oh, and look at you." Laura looked down at Brittany once she was finished hugging Jane. "Jane, it looks like she's grown a foot since I last saw her."

"Yeah, she's had a bit of a growth spurt over the past year," said Jane. She suddenly felt a pang of guilt. Her mother's words reminded her of the fact that she and her daughter hadn't visited very often in the past few years. Once Brittany had started kindergarten a year ago, Jane hadn't needed her parents to watch her daughter anymore. Brittany was able to go to after-school care until Jane got off from work. But still, Jane could have paid her parents more frequent visits. For what it was worth, they had helped take care of Brittany when she was an infant. And despite how strict they had been with Jane, Jane couldn't help but feel that she owed them some involvement in their granddaughter's life.

"Brittany, say hi to your grandmom," said Jane. She knew her daughter to be the shy type around people she hadn't seen in a while. They hadn't visited Jane's parents in going on six months now. "She's just shy, that's all," she told her mom, seeing that Brittany's eyes were still glued to the pavement of the front porch.

"That's perfectly fine," said Laura. "Well, come on in. There's no point in us standing here like this." She moved away from the entrance to allow them room to enter.

Jane nudged Brittany inside first. As she followed her into the house, she could smell the aroma of dinner being cooked. It smelled like beef stew. Were her parents going to expect them to stay for dinner? She figured they might.

"So," said Laura as she shut the door behind them. She turned to Jane. "Is there anything you think Brittany might like to do while we talk?"

Jane became a little uncomfortable. She didn't realize that her parents wanted to have a whole discussion about them lending her money. Were they going to send her on a guilt trip? They'd better not. She'd worked her butt off these past seven years. They'd better cut her some slack.

"She can just watch TV or something," said Jane. "Whatever's easiest."

"You know what?" said Laura. "I think we still have that chalk set. It would be in the basement."

"Oh, the sidewalk chalk?" asked Jane. She remembered how when she would come to pick Brittany up from work she would often see her out on the sidewalk drawing anything and everything. She'd loved that chalk.

"Yeah," said Laura. "Do you think she'd still be interested? It would be a nice way for her to get outside a little today."

Jane knew her mom to be subtle with her words. She never was fond of the idea of Jane bringing Brittany up in an apartment. She'd made it clear to Jane that Brittany should have a neighborhood to run around in, with lots of kids her age to play with. Well, Brittany had gotten that here when she was younger. But Jane wished her parents would just be satisfied for once and mind their own business. She'd proven to them that she could handle being a mother, so why couldn't they just back off? So she didn't finish college; she didn't settle down with a husband and have her daughter that way. She'd made a mistake. If only they could let it go and realize she was doing the absolute best she could as a single mother.

Biting her tongue, Jane looked down at Brittany. "Brittany, honey, do you want to play outside with the chalk?"

Still looking down at the ground, Brittany nodded her head.

"All right then," said Laura. "Well, let me go and make sure it's down in the basement. And why don't you two come on into the kitchen for now?"

"Do I hear company?" came a voice that Jane recognized to be her father's. As she and Brittany followed Laura down the hallway and into the kitchen, they saw him coming up from the basement steps.

"Hi, Dad," said Jane, walking over to her father to give him a hug.

"Hi, Jane," said her father, hugging her back. "It's good to see you again, sweetie."

"And look who we have here." Once he was finished

hugging Jane, Jack looked down at Brittany, who was standing right beside her mother.

"She's a little shy today," said Jane. "Brittany," she said as she looked down at her daughter, "don't you remember Grandpa Jack?"

"Jack," said Laura, stepping in front of Jane and Brittany. "Did you happen to see any chalk down in the basement?"

"Chalk?"

"Yes," said Laura. "For Brittany to play with."

"Well," said Jack. "I really wasn't looking, but—"

"Here, I'll go and look myself." Laura pushed past Jack and headed down the basement steps.

"Well, can I get either of you girls anything to drink?" asked Jack, looking over at Jane and Brittany.

"I'm fine for now, Dad," said Jane.

"And how about you?" Jack bent down, making himself more level with Brittany.

"Brittany, do you want something to drink?" Jane asked her daughter.

Brittany shook her head no.

"Well," said Jack, motioning for the kitchen table that the three of them were standing beside, "let's all sit down."

Jane pulled out the chair nearest her. As she sat down, her father did so as well. Brittany continued to be by Jane's side. Jane figured there was no point in her going to sit down, given that she would probably be going right back outside in a few minutes.

"So how've you been, Jane?" Jack asked.

"I've been doing well, actually," said Jane. "Just financial issues, as you know."

"We've still got them" came Laura's voice.

Jane turned to see her mother coming up the basement steps. She was carrying the chalk set. "Great," she said.

Reaching the top of the steps, Laura handed the chalk set over to Brittany. "Here you go, hon. You have a good time out there."

"What do you say, Brittany?" Jane said to her daughter as she took the chalk from Laura.

"Thank you," said Brittany.

"You're quite welcome," said Laura.

"All right, Brittany," said Jane. "So why don't you go outside and play. Grandma, Grandpa, and I have to have an important discussion."

Brittany obliged, turning and heading back down the foyer to the front door.

"She's so well behaved," said Laura, walking behind Jane to take a seat across from Jack.

"Yeah," said Jane, "she's usually more of a wild child." As she heard the front door open and shut, she realized that it was now time to get down to business. She hoped to God that this would not get ugly.

"So you both know why I'm here," said Jane, bravely beginning the conversation but struggling to look into the eyes of either of her parents.

"Yes, we do, and let me ask you, Jane," began her father, "how did you manage all these years without asking us for a single cent?"

Jane, surprised at the direction in which the conversation was going, responded, "You're not mad?"

"Why would we be mad?" asked her mother.

"Because I haven't lived up to your expectations?"

"Oh, sweetie," said her mother, "that is not at all true.

You've proven to us that you have what it takes to fulfill the responsibility of motherhood. We underestimated you, big time."

"But you guys have helped," said Jane, thinking of the many times over the years that her parents had watched Brittany for her while she was at work.

"Not close to as much as we thought we would have had to," said her father.

"I'm being honest with you, Jane," began her mother. "If I had gotten pregnant at twenty and been forced to drop out of college in order to get a job that pays just over minimum wage, I probably would have lost my mind."

"Then why did you put me through it?" asked Jane.

"Anger, fear that our only child was about to throw her life away," answered her father.

"But weren't you helping to throw my life away by refusing to pay my tuition?"

"We wanted you to take responsibility for your actions," said her father. "We knew that you staying in school and your keeping Brittany, which you insisted on doing, would not have worked."

"But, Mom, you said that you guys underestimated me. If you thought I was going to be a failure by dropping out of college, then why did you make me do that?"

"Jane," said her mother, reaching out to take Jane's hand. "We never expected you to be a failure. We just didn't expect you to be as shockingly independent as you have been."

"We knew that by taking away your college education, you'd learn," added her father. "You're a smart girl. We just expected you to have some troubles along the way."

"Oh, I've had troubles," said Jane, half laughing at how

pathetic things had been for her at times, how it had often taken everything she had in her not to come crying to her parents about how things had been too hard.

"Well, whatever they have been, you've handled them like an adult, because neither your mother nor I have had to get involved."

"So," said her mother in a tone that sounded to Jane like it was time to get down to the crux of the matter. "How much do you need?"

Jane hesitated for a moment, afraid of the reaction her answer would garner. "Is a couple thousand too much?" she asked. She was worried that her parents had a different amount, perhaps a much smaller amount, in mind.

"Nope," said her father. "Just let me go and get my checkbook so I can write you a check."

"Why don't you and Brittany stay for dinner, Jane?" suggested Laura as Jack headed down the foyer to his office. "I've got stew cooking in the crock pot. I think it'll be ready in about ten minutes."

"Okay, we'll do that," said Jane. She was relieved that things had gone so well. She did not expect this from her parents. No criticism, just compliments. Was the apocalypse coming soon? She couldn't be more ecstatic.

After Jane endured a few minutes of small talk with her mother, her father came back into the kitchen and handed her a check for what she could see was two thousand dollars.

"Thank you so much, Dad. I promise you I'll pay you back as soon as I can."

"I know you will," said Jack.

She got her pocket book out of her purse and put the check into it.

"Jane, why don't you go and get Brittany and tell her it's time to wash up for dinner?" Laura told her.

"Sure," said Jane, getting up from the table. She was beginning to feel hungry now. The smell of the food cooking was getting to her system.

She headed down the hallway, and as she opened the front door, along with noticing that it had already begun to get dark, she noticed a man standing over her daughter on the sidewalk, talking to her. She instantly felt guilty for not having thought twice about letting Brittany go outside alone. She shouldn't have allowed it, not if nobody was there supervising.

"Brittany, time for dinner," she announced, interrupting the barely audible conversation between her daughter and the man. As the two of them looked over at her, she stepped down onto the front porch and began walking toward them. She felt it necessary to introduce herself to this man. After all, he'd taken quite an interest in her daughter.

"Hi, I'm Jane, Brittany's mom," she said once she'd gotten through the grass in her parents' front yard and reached the sidewalk. She reached out her hand for the man to shake.

"Oh, so you must be Jack and Laura's daughter," he said, shaking Jane's hand. "I'm Stuart. I live a few houses down from your parents."

"Nice to meet you, Stuart," said Jane. "Brittany." She turned to her daughter. "Go wash up, sweetie."

"I don't want to yet," argued Brittany.

"Then I guess you don't want to watch TV when we get home."

This stopped Brittany from arguing any further. "Fine," she sighed as she gathered up the chalk and put it back in the package. "Bye, Stuart." She waved to the man as she headed toward the house.

"Bye, Brittany," said Stuart. "Your daughter's sure is something, isn't she?" he turned to Jane.

"Yeah, she's something all right," said Jane, rolling her eyes at how stubborn her daughter was whenever she didn't get her way. "Well, it was nice meeting you, Stuart."

"It was nice meeting you, too, Jane," he said. "I hope to see your daughter again sometime."

Jane found this to be a little weird. This was a middle-aged man expressing his interest in spending time with her six-year-old daughter. But she didn't let Stuart know how she felt about what he had just said. Instead, she just smiled.

AFTER DINNER, JANE AND BRITTANY said their good-byes to Laura and Jack as they walked to the car. Once Jane had gotten Brittany settled into the backseat and had gotten into the front, she realized there was something she needed to talk to her daughter about, something that couldn't be put off any longer, despite how much Jane wanted to keep Brittany sheltered from the pain and suffering in the world.

"So you made a new friend today?" asked Jane, turning back to face Brittany.

"Yeah," said Brittany, sounding a little sleepy. It was 8:30, and usually Brittany was in bed by this time. "Stuart was nice," she added.

"Oh, well, what did you guys talk about?" asked Jane. Although Stuart seemed like an okay guy, she needed to confirm through her daughter's response that he wasn't some sort of creep.

"I told him that I'm in first grade and that I wish I was in kindergarten again because it was more fun."

"Oh, okay," said Jane. "Is that all you talked about?"

"I talked about my favorite TV shows and that you don't let me watch some shows because they're for grown-ups."

"Well, Stuart seems like a nice man," said Jane. While she couldn't help but wonder how Brittany had gotten onto these topics with Stuart or if Stuart's purpose in finding these things out about her was anything other than genuine, selfless interest, Jane came to the conclusion that Stuart had probably not been an imminent threat to her daughter. He may have been a little weird, but he didn't seem to be someone Jane needed to be worried about. Not to mention that he was close with Jane's parents. She'd told her parents about him being outside with Brittany, and they'd given no indication that Jane should be concerned. As far as her parents could tell, Stuart was just a single, lonely, middle-aged man searching for human contact wherever he could get it.

Now it was time for the hard part. "Brittany," she began, "there's something I need to talk to you about. Can you listen?"

"What, Mom?" asked Brittany.

How was she going to say this? She would try to leave out as many disturbing details as possible. "Brittany," she began, searching for the right words to say next. "There are some grown-ups who want to capture and hurt little kids. They might do this by promising you candy if you get into their car. So if a stranger ever tells you they have candy and they ask you to go someplace with them to get it, say no and walk away. Do you understand me?"

"But, Mom," said Brittany, "Stuart didn't offer me candy."

Jane laughed at this. She was impressed by how her daughter had made the connection. "I know, honey," she said. "Stuart's a good man. But I still want you to be careful with people you don't know.

"Let me tell you something, Brit. If a grown-up ever tries to kidnap or hurt you and I'm not around to help, I want you to fight that person with all your might. Scream, kick them, bite them, scratch them, hit them—anything you can do to fight them off. And then I want you to run as fast as you can to a safe place and get help. Okay?"

"Okay, Mom," said Brittany, whose seriousness, while it was adorable for someone her age, let Jane know that her daughter had absorbed everything she had just said.

With that, Jane started the car and drove them home.

Eight Years Later

chapter 2

Since the day when Jane had borrowed money from her parents, quite a bit had happened. One thing was that Jane had managed to get a better job working as an accountant in the city. This was, of course, after she'd gone back to college to get her long-lost degree in business. This had meant that she had begun to rely on her parents again to take care of Brittany when she was at night school. The lack of one-on-one time between Jane and her daughter had not been easy, but Jane had been determined to get a better job where she wasn't on a road to nowhere financially. Her job at Giant had had its perks, but she hadn't wanted to keep living paycheck to paycheck. She'd wanted to have the financial means to save up enough money to move out of the apartment she'd been renting and to move into a home in a decent, but hopefully not too pretentious, suburban neighborhood where there were plenty of kids for her daughter to play with. Taking into consideration the advice her mother gave her, she had decided that it was best for Brittany to have a nice childhood where she could run around with other kids as opposed to being cooped up in an apartment where her only forms of entertainment were television and dolls. Jane's job as an accountant made all of this possible.

Brittany had grown up quite a bit over the eight years that had passed. She was now fourteen years old and a freshman in high school. She wasn't a big fan of school, though. It was a social jungle, she felt, and, being as quiet and shy as she was at times, it could be very stressful trying not to be one of the outcasts so many of her friends looked down upon. Fortunately for Brittany, she had little trouble making and keeping friends. People seemed to be drawn to her. Perhaps it was because she was a beautiful girl with long dirty-blonde hair, brownish-green eyes, and a lean body. Several guys had crushes on her; at least that's what her friends had told her.

Brittany's best friend was Claire. Claire was a social climber who was willing to do whatever it took to be a part of the "in" crowd. She would be sure to drag Brittany along with her whenever she saw an opportunity for popularity. For instance, Brittany wasn't interested in partying all that much, but during the summer between middle and high school, the summer that had just passed, Claire had constantly been pressuring Brittany to come to the high school house parties with her. Claire's older brother, Greg, had just graduated from high school back in the spring, and as a jock who had been on the school's varsity football team, needless to say he had been one of the school's biggest hotshots. This had made it easy for Claire to fit right in with the coolest people at Susquehanna Township High.

Brittany had gone to one of the parties with Claire back in July. She'd had to engage in the cliché of sneaking out of her house, knowing full well that her mother wouldn't have allowed her to go. She and Claire had hitched a ride from Greg;

it had been his last party before he'd gone off to college, and he'd wanted to get sloshed.

It had been a stupid idea, riding with Claire in her brother's car, not knowing how she would get home with Greg being too drunk to drive. And to make matters worse, she hadn't known anyone at the party, and neither had Claire really, aside from Greg and his friends. Brittany had been disgusted by all the guys trying to rub up against her in rhythm to the hip-hop music blaring out of the speakers. She'd figured Claire would have felt the same way, but when she'd looked around the room for her, past the crowd of people, she had seen Claire dancing dirty with some guy she knew Claire had never even met before that night. It had only become more uncomfortable when she'd seen Clare walk off with the guy to get cozy with him on one of the couches. Claire ditching her for a guy had not been something Brittany had hoped for in coming to this party, which is why she had taken it upon herself to leave early and walk home.

Claire had understood. House parties weren't for everyone, and Brittany was still cool to her. They'd been friends since the fourth grade, when Brittany had moved into the neighborhood, and they weren't about to quit hanging out just because one of them was a little more reserved than the other. But that didn't mean Claire wouldn't think of other ways to help raise Brittany's social status at Susquehanna Township.

It was a cool fall afternoon as Brittany and Claire walked home together from school. The leaves had begun to fall from the trees, and the cold was making its mark more and more each day. Winter wasn't far off.

"So do you want to come over my house tonight?" Claire asked Brittany as they reached the sidewalk that marked the start of their neighborhood.

"Sure," said Brittany. "What do you want to do? Do you want to, like, watch a movie or order pizza or something?"

"Yeah, we could do that," said Claire. "Or I've got a better idea."

"Oh, and what might that be?" asked Brittany, playing along.

"You promise you won't freak out?"

"Um, okay …" Brittany was curious as to what it was that Claire had in mind.

"Okay, so my parents are going away for the weekend," began Claire. "I think it's some bed and breakfast place somewhere; I don't know. And my brother, when he left for college at the end of the summer, gave me an early birthday present. You want to know what it was?"

"No shit," said Brittany, mocking her friend's way-to-state-the-obvious manner.

"Pot," said Claire.

Brittany wasn't surprised by this. She knew Claire—always trying to fit in, to do what everyone else was doing.

"I've wanted to try it so bad," said Claire, "but my parents haven't gone away in like forever, and I was afraid if we smoked it while they were around, they'd find out."

"I can't believe you haven't tried it already with all the parties you go to."

"Well, I haven't really gone to that many parties lately, and I don't want my first time to be around a bunch of people I don't even know. I mean, what if I start blurting out personal shit?"

Brittany laughed at this. She could picture Claire high, acting like a complete idiot and making a fool out of herself. "So you want me to come over and smoke weed with you tonight?"

"Yeah, that's kind of why I told you, Brittany. Anyway, my brother said it makes you laugh a lot and when it wears off you're really hungry."

"I can't believe your brother gave you weed for your birthday," laughed Brittany as she stopped in front of her house. "I mean, what if your parents found out?"

"Well, he knows I'm good at hiding things from them. So do you want to do it or what?"

"I'll think about it," said Brittany, beginning to debate the positives and negatives of getting high.

"Well, if you decide to, don't come over until after 5:30 because my parents aren't leaving until then. I don't want them getting any ideas."

"Okay," said Brittany. "See you." She headed toward her front door, sliding her book bag off her back so she could get her key out of it.

"I hope you'll come," Claire said to her.

Brittany didn't see her mom's car in the driveway, which meant that she was still at work. As usual, Brittany would be home alone until the evening. She never minded this, though. It was always nice having some alone time after having been around people all day long, with little to no privacy throughout the day.

Brittany closed the door behind her once she was in the house. After hanging her key on the key rack, she took off her shoes and put them by the front door as opposed to in the coat closet where she usually put them. This was assuming she did decide to go to Claire's tonight.

She then headed upstairs to her room, carrying her backpack on her shoulder. It was always a pain for her, climbing the stairs while lugging the heavy load of books and binders only to have to get them out soon after to start her hours of homework. Of course, this was Friday. She could wait until tomorrow or Sunday to start it.

When she got to her room, she set her book bag down on the ground and retrieved her walkman from the book bag's front pouch. She put the headphones over her ears and turned on the walkman, which already had a CD in it. She turned to track 8, Kelly Clarkson's "Walk Away." Aside from "Miss Independent," this was her favorite Kelly Clarkson song. And it was the perfect song for her to be listening to now, to help revive her from a long, exhausting week at school.

As the music began to play, she headed out of her bedroom and started down the upstairs hallway. She wanted to get a soda from the kitchen. She could use some caffeine right now.

"*You've got your mother and your brother every other undercover tellin' you what to say.*" Brittany voiced the lyrics as she danced her way down the steps.

As she got to the bottom of the steps, she headed down the foyer and into the kitchen. She couldn't remember if her mom had put some of the cans of Pepsi in the refrigerator; she hoped so, though. There was nothing like drinking a cold, caffeinated soda right out of the can. No need to worry about ice, which would only water it down.

As she opened the refrigerator door, she was happy to see the neatly placed cans of Pepsi on the top shelf. She grabbed one and shut the refrigerator door.

"*Well if you don't have the answer, why you still standing here?*" After opening the Pepsi, she put the can to her mouth and took a nice, thirst-driven gulp. It was delightful tasting the sweet, sugary liquid as it slid down her throat. It was the perfect pick-me-up.

Heading back through the foyer and upstairs to her room, she sipped the soda along the way so that she wouldn't spill it. Once she was at the top of the steps, she hurried down the hallway to her room, realizing that the song was about to reach its second chorus. She wanted to be ready to dance to it.

Once in her room, she quickly set the can of soda down on her desk right at the time the song reached its chorus. She began to dance, moving her waist from side to side and her head from left to right, allowing her hair to fly in all directions. She loved dancing for fun. It was liberating. It helped free her of all the constraints society placed on a fourteen-year-old.

HE COULD SEE HER THROUGH the blinds that had been pulled all the way up. She was jumping up and down, her hair flying all about. She looked as though she were having the time of her life.

He'd been watching this girl for some time now. She was always alone at this time in the afternoon, right after school let out for the day. He liked this. He liked that there was no one here, no one to get in the way. He wished she was alone like this during the night. The daylight meant people, everywhere.

She had a mother. Obviously she was too young to live alone. But he had never seen a man coming or leaving the house—just a mother.

"Excuse me. Is there a problem, sir?"

The man jolted, instinctively turning around to meet his questioner, who he could see was a middle-aged woman standing across the street beside her mailbox. "No, ma'am," he responded, trying to keep his cool. "Just admiring the design of this house. It's got some great aspects to it."

"Oh," said the woman. "Well, it isn't for sale." He could tell she sensed he was full of it. She more than likely knew the real reason why he was gazing at the house. The girl was very visible, dancing around in her room like she was.

"Well then," said the man. "I guess there's no point in me looking, now, is there?" He took a second before casually walking off, heading toward the edge of the neighborhood where his car was parked. He glanced back at the woman one last time and could see that she had gotten her mail and was heading back into her house. Hopefully, she would forget all about it.

Because he wasn't done with this girl. Not even close. His plans would not be ruined. He'd never done something like this before. He'd always had the urges, but up until now, he'd never followed through with any of his fantasies. But now that he'd found the perfect opportunity to follow through, by God, it would work out just as he saw fit.

chapter 3

B rittany was finishing up her math homework as she glanced at the clock on her desk and saw that it was five of six. Wow, she'd sure lost track of time. Claire was probably figuring she wouldn't show.

She grabbed her backpack sitting beside her desk and pulled her cell phone out of it. She wanted to see if Claire had called or texted her to see what the deal was. As she flipped open her phone, she saw that she had one new message in her inbox. It was from Claire: *r u coming?*

What the heck, Brittany thought to herself. It's not like she had anything better to do that night. And she didn't have to smoke the weed if she didn't want to. And even if she did, it's not like she'd get addicted. It wasn't heroin or anything.

She texted Claire back: *be right over. sorry. lost track of time.* She flipped her phone closed once the text message had been sent.

She closed up her binder and her math textbook and set them side by side on her desk. She'd finish the last few problems when she got home from Claire's. That is, if she wasn't too stoned to think clearly. She realized that she should call her mom to let her know she'd be over at Claire's for the evening. She could do two things at once, though. Getting up out of her desk chair, she flipped her phone back open and, as she headed out of her bedroom, began to dial her mother's cell number. She figured that her mom was working overtime at her job, because usually she was home by now.

But as she headed down the hallway, she heard the front door opening. She flipped her phone closed, realizing there was no point in finishing the call. As she reached the top of the steps, she could see her mom coming in the front door carrying some grocery bags, her purse, and the mail from that day.

"Hi," Brittany said to her as she headed down the steps. "I was just about to call you."

"Yeah, there were a few things we needed in the house," said Jane, shutting the front door and heading through the foyer into the kitchen. "How'd your day go?"

"Good," said Brittany as she got to the bottom of the steps and followed her mom into the kitchen. "I'm going to go over to Claire's. Is that okay?" she asked her mother as Jane began taking items out the grocery bags she'd placed on the kitchen table alongside her purse and the mail.

"I guess," said Jane. "I was hoping we could spend some time together, though, since it's the weekend." She looked over at Brittany as she opened the refrigerator and placed a carton of orange juice on the top shelf.

"We have all Saturday and Sunday," Brittany argued. "And I don't have to spend the night or anything."

"Well ... all right then." Jane sighed, shutting the refrigerator door and returning to the kitchen table to unload the rest of the groceries. "And you're sure Claire's parents are okay with you going over there all the time like you do?"

Oh, that's right. Brittany had forgotten all about the fact that her mom didn't know that Claire's parents were out of town. She probably wouldn't care either way, but she might get suspicious that Brittany and Claire were up to something, all alone in the house like they would be. So it was best to just keep that little detail hidden.

"I don't go over there that much, Mom," she said. "This is the first time I've gone over there this week."

"All right," Jane sighed. "Well, have fun then. And call me if you want a ride home."

"Mom, it's five houses down," said Brittany. Why was her mother being so ridiculous?

"I know, but it'll be dark, and you might not feel safe walking home all by yourself."

"I'll be fine." Brittany wanted to ingrain the sense of security she felt about the situation into her mother's paranoid head. Her mom must have been forgetting all the other times she had left Claire's late at night and gotten home just fine. "And besides, you'll probably be asleep by the time I leave."

"I know, I know," said Jane, putting both hands up, which to Brittany, was her way of surrendering her overprotective demeanor. "I'm just being your mother." She walked over to where Brittany was standing by the entrance to the kitchen. She placed her hands on each of Brittany's shoulders and looked her in the eyes. Brittany had grown to the point where she was only a few inches shorter than her mother. "God, you're getting so grown up." She eyed Brittany up and down. "I can't do anything for you anymore."

Brittany was uncomfortable by this sudden display of affection made by her mother. She became even more uncomfortable when Jane kissed her on the forehead. "Okay,

I have to go," she said, loosening her mother's grasp on her shoulders as she began to head back down the foyer to the front door.

"All right," said Jane. "Have a good time. I love you."

"Okay," said Brittany, not feeling quite comfortable saying "I love you" back. "Okay" was enough. She'd accepted her mother's love, hadn't she?

Once she had her jacket and shoes on, she headed out the front door.

"I KNEW YOU'D COME," SAID Claire, smiling as she held open the front door for Brittany.

"Yeah, sorry again," said Brittany as she stepped inside the house. "I just got caught up in my math homework." She took her jacket off and hung it up on the coat rack by the door, as she was accustomed to doing whenever she came over to Claire's.

"It's no problem," said Claire as she shut the front door and locked it. "We've got all night."

"So follow me." Claire led Brittany most of the way down the foyer before stopping at and opening the door that led down into the basement.

"You want to do it in the basement?" asked Brittany. She wondered why Claire would choose her half-finished basement to get high in when they had the whole house to choose from.

"Yeah," said Claire. "My parents hardly ever come down here. I don't want them smelling it when they get back. They'll flip out."

"Well, go on." Brittany hesitated as Claire held out her arm for Brittany to go down.

"Is it down there already?" Brittany asked. She was beginning to feel a little nervous about all of this. What if something were to go wrong? What if she were to have an allergic reaction to the drug or something? She'd have to go to the hospital, and the doctors would find it in her system—and she'd probably be expelled from school because of it.

"Yeah, it's down there, Brittany. That's why I don't have it with me right now." Claire rolled her eyes.

Brittany remained hesitant.

"You're having second thoughts, aren't you?" she asked. The look of disappointment on Claire's face was more than visible to Brittany, but she didn't know what to say to her friend. She wanted to do this, but at the same time, she feared the possible risks.

"One smoke isn't going to kill you."

"I know," said Brittany, irritated at how pathetic Claire had just made her out to be. "I'm just, like, worried if something were to go wrong ..."

"Oh my God," said Claire in aggravation. "Brittany, it's weed, not freaking cocaine."

"I'm just worried if someone was to find out, we could get into a lot of trouble."

Claire sighed. "You know what? We don't have to do it. I'm just trying to be your friend here, that's all. But if you'd rather just play it safe in every little detail of your life, then whatever."

"All right." Brittany didn't like hearing this from Claire. The last thing she wanted was to become someone who played it safe all her life. "I'll do it."

"Thank God!"

"So is it just going to, like, relax us?"

"Yeah, and you *need* to relax. I haven't forgotten about how you were earlier this week."

"Oh God, yeah," Brittany laughed. She remembered how angry she had gotten when venting to Claire about how school was overwhelming her. Looking back, it made her feel kind of embarrassed.

"So you ready?" asked Claire consolingly.

Brittany laughed, shaking off her nerves. "Okay," she said. Upon Claire's request, she led the way down into the basement.

JANE TOOK A SIGH OF relief as she finally sat down at the table to eat. She couldn't wait to dig in. She was starved, not having eaten since her lunch break at work, which was at noon.

The Lean Cuisine cheese ravioli was delicious, just what she needed after a long week at work. The glass of red wine was great too. This was a fine enough way for her to spend her Friday night. She'd eat her dinner and then just watch some television until she felt tired enough to go to sleep. It was the way she'd been spending most of her Fridays since she'd had Brittany, and it was no bother to her. She didn't see why everyone felt the urge to go out on Friday nights. She was worn out by this time of the week, and she wondered how everyone else managed to be so wide awake and excited.

Of course, this probably applied to teenagers more than it did to adults in their midthirties like her. Admittedly, she'd gone along with it as a teenager, but still, Jane didn't get why Friday had to be such a big deal. Did people really hate their weekday lives that much? And if so, didn't they realize they'd be getting right back into it the following Monday, which was really in no time at all?

Jane liked her job, as rigorous and tedious as it was at times. It was fulfilling. It gave her a sense of accomplishment to work with her individual clients, making sure that their financial statements were correctly prepared and reported. On occasion, she'd get a really difficult client who never seemed to be satisfied, but overall, she was content doing what she was doing. And the salary was great. She'd never expected, as a single mom, to have been able to afford a two-story house like this one. But she'd done it. She was proud of herself. She'd proven to the world that, while getting pregnant was a mistake, she didn't need a man to help her do what she as a woman could very well do herself.

As she helped chase down her second bite of ravioli with a sip of wine, Jane decided she ought to check the mail. She reached across the table and began to sort through it as she ate. There were three envelopes and a catalog from L. L. Bean. Why did she keep getting these catalogs? She'd gotten Brittany's book bag from them, but that was a few years ago. L. L. Bean was too formal for her taste, not to mention expensive—

Jane's muscles tensed up. Out of the corner of her eye, she caught something coming from right outside of the left sidelight to her front door. As she turned her head and peered down the hallway, she saw that there was no longer anything there.

She breathed a sigh of relief. It must have just been the shadow of a car driving by. That happened a lot.

But she still wanted to make sure. She got up and headed down the hallway to the front door. When she got there, she flipped on the light switch for the front porch. She then slouched down to peer out the sidelight, and as she expected, she saw nothing.

She was being ridiculous. Did she honestly think there had

been a person out there looking into her home? As far as she knew, this neighborhood had never experienced any break-ins. She was just being her usual paranoid self.

As she stood back up, she saw that Brittany's key was still on the key rack. She was relieved to know that in case she fell asleep (which she didn't feel right doing, knowing that Brittany was going to be walking home alone late at night), Brittany knew about the spare key on the back porch under the flowerpot.

Jane left the outside light on and made sure that the front door was locked before returning to the kitchen to finish her dinner. Despite her sense of security that nothing was wrong at the moment, she knew that she could never be too sure.

Brittany and Claire sat on the floor on either side of the wooden coffee table surrounded by two couches and a television set. Brittany watched as her friend took her first hit.

As Claire took the joint from her mouth, she began to cough. "Holy shit," she gasped. "This is so strong." Her eyes were beginning to water.

"What does it feel like?" asked Brittany, wide-eyed.

"There's only one way to find out," answered Claire, handing the joint over to Brittany.

Brittany took it from Claire and eyed it for a second. *Here goes nothing,* she thought. *My first illegal drug use.* She put the joint to her mouth and inhaled. As soon as she did so, she began to cough even more violently than her friend had.

Claire laughed at Brittany's intense reaction to the weed. "Are you okay?" she asked.

Brittany nodded while trying to settle her coughing. When she did settle it down, she handed the joint back to Claire.

Claire took the joint from her, taking another drag. "You know who you reminded me of just then?" she told Brittany.

"Who?" asked Brittany, taking the joint again from Claire. She hesitated before giving it another go. She made sure not to inhale so deeply this time.

"Mrs. Freeman," said Claire. "You know how she has those coughing attacks in the middle of class sometimes? Brad told me he saw a big wet spot near her crotch one time."

"Oh, thanks, Claire," said Brittany, who was relieved that the weed hadn't caused her to break out into a second coughing attack. She handed the joint to Claire. "That's exactly who I want to remind people of."

"Hey, well, at least you're not a bitch like her." Claire took the joint from Brittany. "I mean, it pisses me off that she gives us those essays to write at the end of class. It's like, how does she expect us to finish? And then she goes and gives us that checks and balances test when she didn't even bother to teach us the shit. 'If you'd studied hard enough, you'd have done well.' God, she's such a bitch."

Brittany had keeled over, laughing at Claire's impression of their teacher. Sometimes, when their teacher talked, it looked as though she had no teeth. And the way Claire just imitated her—it was dead on and hilariously so.

Or maybe it wasn't all that funny. Because right now, everything was starting to seem funny. This probably meant one thing only: that the weed was starting to get to her.

JANE WAS UPSTAIRS IN HER bathroom, brushing her teeth. She still had her work clothes on. She didn't want to get into her pajamas yet because she was afraid the comfort of them would make her too sleepy to wait up for Brittany.

When she finished brushing her teeth, she rinsed off the toothbrush, put it in its holder, and then bent down to rinse her mouth out under the sink. Once she could no longer taste the toothpaste in her mouth, she turned off the faucet and dried her mouth with the towel she had next to the sink.

She looked at her reflection in the mirror as she set the towel down. While she could tell that her skin was beginning to look noticeably older, she was happy to see that there was still no sign of wrinkles. She knew that they were bound to come eventually, though. Both of her parents had noticeable wrinkles, and wasn't it hereditary? At least she took good care of herself. She didn't smoke or go tanning or spend a lot of time out in the sun. So she felt secure that her skin would stay wrinkle-free for plenty of time still.

Then again, why was she so caught up in how she looked? It's not like she was trying to get a boyfriend anytime soon. And even if she did decide to date, she'd make sure the man wasn't some shallow guy who she'd have to keep up appearances for. He'd need to accept her for who she was, for how old she was. And he'd have to get along well with Brittany too.

She'd better go downstairs now, she figured. She'd just watch TV some more while waiting for Brittany to come home. What was it, 9:00 now? Brittany probably wouldn't be over there too much longer. And if she was, Jane would call her to see if she'd decided to spend the night. Hopefully, Brittany would be considerate enough to call her, though, if that was the case.

Jane turned the bathroom light off, and as she stepped into her bedroom, she froze, feeling like her heart was about to stop.

Standing at the entrance to her bedroom, lit up by the hallway light, was a man wearing a ski mask.

"Oh my God," said Jane, trying to catch her breath. As soon as she finished saying this, the man came at her.

"Please, no!" she pleaded as she ran back into the bathroom, hoping there would be enough time for her to close the door and lock it. She knew that this was her only option. There was no way she could get to the phone. It was across the room, and if she tried to retrieve it, he would catch her before she even had a chance to pick it up. In the bathroom, she knew she was going to have to jump out of the window. The fall would hurt, but she'd rather sprain her ankle than fall victim to whatever horrible things this man had in mind for her.

Feeling that her fright was causing her body to move in slow motion, Jane made a move to close the bathroom door and lock it, hoping to God she would be fast enough.

But she wasn't. The man forced his way in, knocking Jane to the ground in the process as the door hit her hard in the face. She wanted to scream for help, but she was silenced by the pain of the blow.

Jane could feel the blood beginning to run out of her nose as the man turned the bathroom light on. She could see, through the slits of his ski mask for his eyes and his mouth, that he was white, as though this made any difference. The truth of the matter was that he did not want her to know who he was. Could this mean that he only intended to rape her?

She knew there was no way she could get out of the bathroom window now. The blinds were shut, and the window was locked. There wouldn't be enough time. She had to find another way to escape.

The scissors. She had a pair of them on the bathroom

countertop in the wicker basket over in the corner. Would she have time to grab them and stab him with them?

She could see that he was reaching inside of the coat he was wearing. To her horror, he was pulling out a knife. He wasn't going to rape her. He was going to kill her. She had to get the scissors. Fast.

Seeing her reach up onto the countertop, for what he did not know, the man jumped down onto her, knocking her back down onto the floor. He then raised the knife and plunged it into her chest.

Jane screamed out in pain. The feeling of the knife sinking into her flesh carried with it more pain than she could ever have imagined. Still, she thought of the scissors. Could she fight this man off and still get to them? Or if not the scissors, could she at least fight him off and make a run for it? Was there still enough strength left in her?

The man withdrew the knife from her chest and drove it right back in.

Jane knew that she was going to die now. She knew that she wasn't going to get to the scissors. As she felt the agony of the knife being withdrawn from her chest a second time and saw the man raising the knife back into the air, she knew that he was going to continue stabbing her until she was dead. She knew that Brittany was going to come home and find her dead like this. And was this man going to kill Brittany too? As she felt the knife sink into her chest a third time, she knew that there was nothing she could do but let this man's sinister plan be put into effect. And if that meant killing her daughter, too, then that is what would happen.

She began to feel herself slipping out of consciousness. The wetness saturating her body she knew to be her own blood. It was discomforting. But all she could do now was think of what was to come. She would be no more in this life. It would be over for her very soon.

Moments later, after multiple stab wounds, she slipped away completely. The man had stabbed her to death.

Temporarily relieved of his urges, he breathed heavily, exhausted from the intensity of what he had just done. He forced himself up from the floor and, seeing the hand towel beside the sink, used it to wipe the blood from his knife before sliding it back into the inside pocket of his jacket.

He then walked out into the bedroom, leaving the bathroom light on behind him.

chapter 4

It was nearly 11:00 as Brittany stood on the front porch to Claire's house, saying her good-byes to her friend before heading back home.

"We have to do this again," said Brittany, laughing in acknowledgment of what an amazing time she had just had. She was so glad she'd decided to smoke the weed. She hadn't had so much fun since she was a little kid. The best part was when Claire had put on the music and they'd gotten up and danced around the basement, falling into one another in the stoned, clumsy state that they'd both been in. That had been a blast.

"We will," said Claire reassuringly. "Oh, you know what? Wait a second." She ran back into the house.

"What is it?" asked Brittany.

"I'll be right back," she could hear Claire saying from in the house.

Brittany felt a little giggly still, like she could burst out laughing right now. Maybe it was the fresh air too. That always made her feel good, especially when it was brisk like it was tonight.

After a minute or so, Claire came back out with a bottle of perfume. "Here, spray this on yourself," she said, handing it over to Brittany. "You don't want your mom to smell anything."

"Well, she might wonder why I have perfume on," said Brittany, taking the perfume bottle. "But still, I'm glad you thought of this." She gave a few spritzes here and there on her clothes. She didn't think her mom would get all that angry if she found out, but she didn't want to risk it.

When she was done, she handed the bottle back to Claire.

"Sorry you can't spend the night," Claire said to her as she took the bottle from her.

"Yeah, I know," said Brittany. "It's just that I told my mom I was coming home. She's been complaining that I haven't been spending enough time with her." She rolled her eyes.

"No, it's cool," said Claire. "I'm just glad I have this weekend away from *my* parents."

"Yeah, and I just need to take a shower and stuff." Brittany hadn't had the time to take one the previous night because she'd had so much homework and had been up until after midnight working on it.

"Well, I'm really glad we did this, Brittany."

"Yeah, I know. And maybe you can come over and hang out with my mom and me tomorrow." She felt bad about leaving Claire by herself the entire weekend.

"Um ..."

Brittany laughed. "It sounds stupid, doesn't it?"

"No, it's just I think I'm supposed to go to the movies with Summer tomorrow."

"Oh, okay." Brittany knew that Claire had a lot of friends who were just Claire's friends. Brittany didn't always see eye to eye with some of the girls in their high school. A lot of them were just too superficial and boring for her to get along with.

"But I'll tell them how much fun we had tonight."

"Great," Brittany laughed. "All right, well, have a good rest of your weekend."

"You too."

"Bye." Brittany stepped off the porch and headed home.

WHEN SHE REACHED HER FRONT yard, Brittany reached into her pants pocket for the key and realized that she didn't have it with her. *No big deal*, she thought. She could always get the spare. She knew it was somewhere in the backyard, but she wasn't sure of its exact location. Her mom had told her it was under one of the flowerpots, but there were several of them.

But first, before going to all of that trouble, she'd check to see if the door was unlocked. Maybe her mom had forgotten to lock it. Or maybe she'd left it unlocked on purpose if she'd noticed that Brittany had left her key on the key rack.

She walked up the driveway and down the pathway to her front porch.

Lo and behold, when she tried the doorknob, it was unlocked. The doorknob felt a little loose, though. She figured it needed to be fixed. Maybe the screws were coming out. She'd tell her mom about it this weekend once she'd gotten a good night's rest.

She opened the door and stepped inside the house, flipping the switch to turn off the porch light before shutting the door behind her and locking it. At least the door still locked okay.

She could see that the hallway light was on upstairs as she removed her shoes and hung her jacket back up in the coat closet. She wondered if her mom was still awake. She didn't want to wake her up, though, by shouting up the stairs for her to tell her she was home.

She started up the stairs, smelling her clothes to make sure they didn't wreak of pot still. They weren't too bad. The perfume covered it up pretty well, but she'd still be sure to do her laundry herself this weekend, just in case her mother was to catch the slightest whiff.

As she reached the top of the steps, she realized that she needed to brush her teeth and wash her face. She was so tired, though. She just wanted to plop into bed and fall asleep. Well, she'd get into her pajamas first and then she'd head back down the hallway to the guest bathroom that she called her own, considering that they never had any guests over. Except for Claire, but she always slept in Brittany's bedroom with her as opposed to the guest bedroom that no one ever occupied.

She could see that her mom's bathroom light was on as she reached the end of the hallway, about to head into her room. She peered inside the bedroom and saw that her mom wasn't in bed. She hadn't even gotten into bed; it was still made from the morning. She didn't hear any noise coming from the bathroom, though. The shower wasn't on. Nor was the sink running.

"Mom, I'm home," Brittany called to her.

No response.

"Mom."

Still nothing.

Brittany was beginning to feel a knot tighten in her stomach. Was something wrong with her mom? Why wasn't she responding? She couldn't have been downstairs. All of the lights were off down there.

What was going on? Was she just overreacting? Was the weed making her paranoid?

She stepped into the bedroom and headed toward the bathroom to see what the problem was. If her mom was lying on the floor unconscious, she'd be ready to call 9-1-1.

When she reached the bathroom and peered inside, she lost it. The sight was horrifying. It was the worst thing she had ever seen in her life. And it was real and right in front of her.

She could see her mother lying on the floor with a pool of blood surrounding the upper half of her body. The shirt she was wearing was saturated with her blood. There were punctures around her chest—stab wounds. Her head was tilted to the side, and her eyes were open; they were filled with fear.

She was dead. Her mom was dead. She had been gruesomely murdered.

Brittany began to cry out of helplessness. Her mom was gone, and there was nothing she could do about it. She would never be able to be with her mom again as long as she lived.

Overcome by emotional anguish, Brittany was not prepared for what happened next. She didn't know what to do upon seeing the man stepping out of the closet and walking over to the bedroom door and shutting it. He was trapping her so she couldn't escape. He was going to kill her too.

Brittany felt her body go numb from fear as the masked man came at her. She thought about running into the bathroom, but she knew there was not enough time to close the door behind her.

He had been here waiting for her all night, waiting for her to come home. Who was this man? And how long had he been planning this?

Brittany cowered in fear as the man grabbed hold of her.

Feeling the leather from one of his gloves as he grasped her arm, she knew that she was at his mercy and that whatever he had in store for her was not going to be good. She was going to live out her worst nightmares now. And then it was going to be over for her, just like it was for her mom.

The man dragged her over to the bed and threw her onto it, face up. He then climbed up onto the bed and got on top of her. "Please," Brittany sobbed. "Please don't hurt me." She felt completely helpless. She knew that she should fight back, but the pain of seeing her mother dead like that had defeated her. And the fright of being attacked by this man was overtaking her. She was beginning to retreat, to lose touch with reality. It was too much to bear. She just couldn't take it.

She thought of death, of how she would be at peace once this was all over. This didn't stop her, however, from feeling the man reach for her pants and unbutton them. Despite her knowledge that it would eventually be all over, she knew that he was going to rape her first. She knew that he was going to put himself inside of her. He was going to take away her virginity.

Once he'd unbuttoned her pants, she felt him go for the zipper. When he'd gotten it all the way down, he grabbed hold of both sides of her pants to pull them off of her.

Brittany thought she'd accepted what was about to happen. She'd felt that there was nothing she could do about it, that if she tried to run away, he'd catch up to her and kill her. But as she felt her pants being pulled down off of her waist, she began to feel otherwise. She began to feel what it was going to be like to be raped by this man, how exposed and violated she was going to feel, how ruined she was going to feel. And she didn't want this to happen. She didn't want to die like this. This was not going to be a quick, torture-less death. And her instincts were not okay with this. *She* was not okay with this.

"Get off of me!" She flung her arms at him, hitting him all over, hoping that it would be enough to get him off of her so she could get away. As she hit at him, she felt her anger coming to. She hadn't been angry at first; she'd been too horrified and upset. But she was now beginning to gain perspective on the reality of what was happening. Her mom had been killed, and now this man was going to kill her once he'd raped her. She valued her life too much to allow this to happen. She valued her life too much to allow him to take it away from her.

She didn't seem to be strong enough, though. He had to be nearly twice her size. She sank punches into his rib cage, his arms … she even tried to knee him in the groin. But he was still on top of her, still in complete control.

The face! She ought to try hitting him in the face. That would have to hurt him, at least a little. Quickly reaching her arm up before he could have a chance to pin it down, with all her might she sank a punch into the side of his head.

To her immense relief, she felt him loosen his hold on her as he groaned in pain. It had worked. "Get off of me!" Brittany screamed at him again, this time almost excitedly. The adrenaline was beginning to rush through her. She was beginning to feel herself taking control like she never had before. She was proud to see that punching him in the head had affected him. But it wasn't over yet. He still had hold of her legs. He was still yanking at her pants, trying to get them down even further.

Brittany knew she needed to make the next punch count. Clenching her fist, she sent him another blow to the side of his head.

She was thrilled to see that he was yet again impacted by her punch. She took full advantage of his pain and freed herself out from under him. She knew she didn't have much time before he recovered. She had to be fast, as fast as she possibly could be, only faster.

As she crawled as far back onto the bed near the pillows as she could, pulling her pants back up as she did so, he jumped at her, grabbing hold of her leg again. But as she moved further to the side of the bed to attempt to jump off, she freed it from his grip.

The second she was off the bed, she ran to the door, flinging it open and running out of the bedroom. She felt like her heart was going to beat out of her chest as she ran down the hallway faster than she'd ever run in her life. Making the sharp turn for the stairs was extra difficult, considering how fast she was going. But she managed it without hitting the wall. As she started down the steps, she could see him running down the hallway after her. He was right on her tail. If she wasn't quick enough, he'd catch her, and who knows what he would do to her if that happened?

As she raced down the steps, she prayed to God that she wouldn't fall and that she would get out of this house in time before he caught up to her.

When she got to the bottom of the steps, she ran to the door, knowing that she still had to get it open. "Come on, come on." She fiddled with the doorknob, unlocking it. She could hear him on the steps. It sounded like he was close to the landing. One more second and it would be too late.

She turned the doorknob, feeling an intense amount of relief as it swung open.

She darted out of the house, dashing through her front

yard before turning and running up the street. *"Help me!"* she screamed, hoping that someone would come out of their house and save her from this man who she assumed to be chasing after her still. *"Help me! Help me! Heelp meee …"*

chapter 5

The dim light from outside shone in through the windows of Jack and Laura's home. The cloudy day fit well with the mood in the family room.

Brittany sat in between her grandmother and grandfather on the couch. Across from her and her grandparents, sitting on the other couch, was a detective with a pad and pen in his hand. On the coffee table in between the couches was the recorder the detective had set on play.

"So you said there was a light on upstairs when you got home?" asked the detective.

"Yes," said Brittany.

The detective saw that Brittany wasn't looking up at him. She had her head down; her eyes were on her knees. He couldn't possibly imagine what kind of hell this girl was in. He'd seen the hell all the time, but he'd never been through it himself.

He could see that the grandparents also looked in a state of despair. The grandmother, who had her hand on Brittany's knee, was a ghostly pale. Her eyes were filled with tears. The grandfather sat up straight just like a soldier would. He looked calm and collected, but the detective knew that his calm look was only a façade put forth to prevent him from breaking down. He also knew, as a father and soon-to-be grandfather, that the man of the house needed to keep his cool no matter what. He needed to be strong for the rest of the family.

After jotting down some notes in his pad, the detective looked back up at Brittany to continue with the questioning. "And then you went upstairs?"

"Yes," answered Brittany, who the detective could see was still looking down at her knees.

"Can you tell me what happened next?"

After a few seconds' pause, Brittany gave him an answer. "I went into my mother's room because her bathroom light was on," said Brittany.

"You wanted to see her and tell her you were home?" asked the detective.

"Yes. And she didn't answer me so I wanted to see if she was okay."

"So you went into the bathroom?"

"Yes."

"And then what?" He was pretty sure he knew the answer to this, but he wanted to hear it from her. Just in case he was wrong, he didn't want to be making assumptions.

"I saw her."

"You saw your mother?"

"Yes. She was dead." She now looked up from her knees and gazed in his direction. She didn't look at him, though. Rather, she stared into space, deep in the pains of what had happened.

The detective now saw the tears beginning to roll down the grandmother's face. This seemed to be just as bad, if not worse, for her as it was for Brittany. She'd lost her daughter.

To think of what it would be like to lose one of his sons … the detective couldn't imagine the tremendous amount of pain it would bring him.

Rubbing his forehead, he looked down at the notes he had been taking. There was still a lot of ground to cover, still a lot of questions he needed to ask her. He hoped she would be able to handle it. Reliving these kinds of experiences, especially one as rare and frightening as this, was not an easy thing to do.

"So," he said, "you saw your mother's body. What then?"

"He came out of the closet." He noticed a change in her voice as she said this. It became weaker, her words slurred somewhat. This was obviously beginning to upset her.

"He came at me and forced me on the bed." She now sounded like she was about to cry. And he could see how horrified her grandmother looked upon hearing this. She had her hands together at her chin. Her eyes were on the ceiling. She was shaking her head in denial, as though she was begging God for this not to be true. The grandfather wasn't looking too good either. He was beginning to lose his composure, his arms beginning to shake, his eyes beginning to fill with tears. This wasn't any easier for him.

"So he forced you onto the bed …" He knew this next question was going to be tough, not as much for Brittany, perhaps, as it would be for her grandparents.

"Did he try to rape you?"

She was beginning to shake now. "I don't want to do this," she said, almost to herself. Her eyes returned to her knees as she shook her head from side to side. "I don't want to do this." Her shaking was worsening, and her breathing was becoming heavier. It looked to the detective like she was starting to hyperventilate.

"Brittany, it's okay, sweetie," said her grandmother, taking Brittany in her arms. "It's okay."

As Brittany rested her head in her grandmother's bosom, she began to cry, loud groans accounting for her sobs. It was at this point that the detective knew that no further progress would be made today.

"I think that's enough for today, detective," the grandfather said to him, pulling himself up off the couch as his crying wife held their traumatized granddaughter. "I'll walk you to the door."

The detective hesitantly forced himself up from the couch, grabbing his recorder off the coffee table and pushing it to stop. He'd have to wait a while before he could rely on Brittany to build on this case. In the meantime, he could visit her neighborhood and see if any of the neighbors had seen anything suspicious.

Present Day

chapter 6

It's a beautiful spring day outside of the Hall Auditorium at Oberlin College. The sun shines brightly in the clear blue sky. It enhances the colors of the trees and flowers surrounding the auditorium. The birds can be heard happily chirping as they fly around the campus. It is a peaceful time of year, a time of awakening.

Inside the Hall Auditorium, an acting class is in session. Up on center stage are a young man and woman, reciting their lines from the copies of the play that each of them holds in their hands.

"You picked me?" says the young man.

"I did,'" says the young woman. "I've been sitting at that desk watching all the salesmen go by, day in, day out. But you've got such a sense of humor, and we do have such a great time together, don't we?" She is trying to talk in the accent for which she thinks the woman would have had, being from Boston, but she feels she isn't doing too well at it.

"Sure, sure." The young man awkwardly takes her in his arms. "Why do you have to go now?"

"It's two o' clock …"

"No, come on in!" He now pulls her toward him.

"My sisters'll be scandalized." She tries not to burst out laughing at this line. "When'll you be back?"

"Oh, two weeks about. Will you come up again?"

"Sure thing. You do make me laugh. It's good for me." She gently squeezes his arm and aims her lips as close as possible to his without allowing them to touch. She makes a smooching noise while at the same time quickly backing away. She realizes that this was a mistake due to her awkwardness and assumes that her professor has probably taken notice. "And I think you're a wonderful man."

"You picked me, heh?"

"Sure. Because you're so sweet. And such a kidder." She makes a hand gesture, trying to add effect.

"Well, I'll see you next time I'm in Boston."

"I'll put you right through to the buyers."

The actor awkwardly reaches out and taps her butt and says, "Right. Well, bottoms up!"

The actress isn't comfortable with this. "Okay," she says in a forfeiting way. She moves away from the actor and looks down off the stage and into the third row of center seating, where her professor is seated. "I can't do this," she says.

The actor looks at her, and it is obvious to her that he is in agreement.

"Why not?" the professor asks her sternly.

"It's just really awkward," the actress says. "I mean, for one thing, Kyle's gay." She doesn't like how her friend's role is pressuring him into being something he's not. "And then, like, we're not even the same age as these people."

The professor lets out a frustrated sigh. "Amanda, I have been through this with you so many times. The key to acting is that you're supposed to *become* the character. Become the person you're portraying and leave whoever you are outside of this class behind."

"It's okay, Amanda," Kyle whispers to her.

"I know," Amanda says to Kyle, hoping she can just reconcile the whole thing.

"So take it from the top," says the professor, rubbing his forehead. "And you both realize you need to have these lines memorized when we get back from break?"

"Yeah," says Kyle.

"Yes," says Amanda. She knows they'll have to be spending a lot of time working on these lines over break. *Fortunately, though, they'll be together—*

"Can I say something?" asks a young woman in the seats. She is back behind everyone a little ways, sitting alone on the inner end of side seats. This causes everyone to turn to her.

"Yes, Brittany?" says the professor.

Brittany feels her heart beginning to beat faster. She always forgets how nerve-wracking it can be to contradict a teacher, especially when the whole class is right there watching her. "I mean, I get what you're saying, professor, about becoming the character and everything. But I honestly can't see Kyle as Willy Loman."

"How about we let Kyle decide what he wants?" the professor tells her. This is a blow to her esteem. But she knows Kyle. He's one of her best friends, and she can't see why he would want to be playing some macho, heterosexual guy he can hardly even relate to. Unless he wants to prove that he's a great actor or something.

"It doesn't matter to me," she hears Kyle say. "I just like acting, so I'll take whatever I can get."

Brittany isn't buying it. She knows he's just trying to avoid what could very well become a tense class environment.

"You see?" she says. "That's the thing. It's kind of ironic. I mean, you've got all these gay men in theater, but they're being forced to play straight roles. It just doesn't make any sense." She sees that her classmates have their eyes on her. Are they with her on this or are they seeing her as some crazy person with a radical agenda? She hopes the former.

"Are you finished, Brittany?" The professor is looking over at her. She can tell that he is pissed off at her. "Because between you and Amanda, we've lost what?"—she sees him gazing at his watch—"a good couple minutes of class time over a petty argument when it's already been stated by Kyle himself that he is okay with playing Willy Loman."

"I don't think it's petty, though." Brittany is surprised at her determination to speak her mind. Since when did she become so outspoken? "I mean, I think it's pretty important for us to be able to play roles that reflect who we are to an extent. But in most plays, there's just the stereotypical male and female roles."

The professor sighs. She can tell that she has made him reconsider.

"I have to be honest," he says. "You do make a valid point, Brittany. And luckily, we're in a time where society is much more accepting of diversity than back when *Death of a Salesman* was written." He pauses. "And who knows? Years from now, there very well may be a large number of mainstream plays that include gay roles.

"Unfortunately," she sees him glance down at his watch, "it looks like we're out of time. Enjoy your spring break everyone.

And when we get back, I expect for you all to have your lines for the first act *memorized*."

"THAT WAS REALLY AWESOME WHAT you said in there, Brittany," Kyle says to Brittany as she, Amanda, and Kyle walk side by side down the hallway just outside of the theater.

"Oh, so you do care," Brittany tells him. "I thought so."

"Yeah, I just didn't want to stir anything up with our teacher."

"But seriously though," says Amanda. "You should be able to play a character that you can relate to."

"I know," says Kyle. "It's such bullshit. And he can't even fucking admit that he doesn't have roles for me. Like, what the hell?

"But on a brighter note," he goes on to say, hoping he can lighten the mood, "are you guys excited about tomorrow?"

"Hell yeah," says Amanda.

"Definitely," says Brittany. "Ever since Jennifer showed us those pictures last week, I've just been counting the days."

"Yeah, it's an awesome place," says Kyle. "And it's literally in the middle of nowhere. I think the nearest house is like five minutes away by car."

"Damn," says Brittany. "And I've actually never really been up in the mountains before. So it's probably going to be really awesome for me."

"Yeah," says Kyle. "I told you guys I went up there when Jennifer and I were dating."

"Yeah, and her whole family came along and ruined it for you both," laughs Amanda.

"Well, they just made it awkward. But it's not like we were going to have sex or anything."

"Okay, I did not need to know that," says Amanda.

Brittany laughs.

"Anyway," says Kyle, "when we went up there, it was just completely mind-blowing for me. It's just like, I didn't realize how big everything was. It was so overwhelming, but in a good way."

"Wow," says Brittany. "Like seriously, I'm so glad I'm friends with you, Kyle."

"Do you think it might be a little awkward though?" asks Amanda.

"Why would it be awkward?" asks Kyle.

"Since Jennifer's bringing her boyfriend," says Amanda.

"Seriously, Amanda?" says Kyle. "Nick knows that I'm gay. Jennifer told him we were dating because I thought I was bisexual, but then I realized I just like guys. Hence, Jeff."

"I guess I just worry about stupid stuff too much," says Amanda.

"Yeah, no kidding," Kyle says to her.

As they approach the end of the hallway and head out the doors into the sunlight, Brittany prepares to part ways with her friends. As usual, she will be heading to her dorm while Kyle and Amanda head to their next classes. She'll be meeting back up with them tonight along with the other three to discuss last-minute details for the trip.

BRITTANY SITS ON THE SIDE of her bed in her dorm room as she talks to her grandmother on her cell phone. "I know, Grandmom," she says. "I miss you too. I—" Her grandmother interrupts. When it sounds like she is done talking, Brittany begins to say something, but once again, her grandmother cuts her off. She just smiles, seeing no point in getting aggravated.

Finally, after her grandmother is done talking about how much she misses her, Brittany is able to get a word in. "I really want to visit you guys," she says. "It's just that I promised my friends I'd hang out with them over break, but I can try to leave a few days early or something so I can see you guys ... We're going up to the mountains. My friend Kyle has an ex-girlfriend whose parents are letting us use their vacation house ... You know about Kyle. I showed you pictures of him.

"But anyway, summer break starts in less than two months, so if I don't get to see you guys during break, it won't be too long before I'm coming back home anyway. And I really do miss you guys."

Her grandmother speaks again, and it sounds to Brittany as if her strategy of mentioning summer break has worked, because her grandmother is moving onto another subject, one that catches Brittany off guard a bit.

"I think I remember her," she says. "Why? ... Oh, that's weird. I hardly even knew her ... How'd she even get your number? ... Yeah, let me get it." She gets off of the bed and walks across the room to where her desk is. She sits down at her chair and retrieves a Post-it and a pen. "Okay, I'm ready." She jots down a phone number. "Okay. So I guess I'll give her a call. Do you have any idea what she wants? ... All right, well, I'll talk to you soon, then ... Love you too. Bye."

She ends the call and goes back to sitting on her bed. She holds the Post-it in her hand, staring at it for a while, debating whether or not to call the number written on it. She knows what this could very well be about, but she also knows it might have to do with something else entirely.

She decides to make the call. She needs to know why this person is so interested in talking to her. Once she's dialed the number, it begins to ring. It rings three times before she hears someone pick up on the other line. "Hello?" says a woman. Brittany figures it must be her.

"Hi" says Brittany, her heart pounding. "Is this Anne Lenin?"

"Yes, this is her," says the woman. "Who's calling?"

"This is Brittany Taylor."

Anne doesn't say anything in response. Brittany wonders if she has caught her off guard by calling her like this. Perhaps she has shocked the woman.

"I used to live across the street from you," Brittany adds, breaking the uncomfortable silence. "I was just talking with my grandmom, and she said you had called and asked to speak with me."

"That's correct," says Anne. Her voice sounds a little shaky.

There is an awkward pause. Brittany doesn't know if she should speak or if she should wait for Anne to say something.

Anne is the one to break the silence this time. "I suppose you wouldn't believe me, Brittany, if I told you I want you to come for a visit. That is, considering how little we knew of one another."

"Do you *want* me to come for a visit?" asks Brittany, not knowing exactly how she should respond to what Anne has just said.

"Yes," says Anne. "That *is* what I want. But I think it's only fair that I tell you why."

"Okay," says Brittany, anticipating the ulterior motive behind her old neighbor's sudden friendliness toward her.

"It's …" she hears Anne hesitating. She can't seem to get the words out.

"What is it?" asks Brittany, feeling like she already knows the answer.

"It's about what happened five and a half years ago."

Brittany knew that this is what it was coming to, from the second her grandmother told her about Anne. She knew there was no other reason for Anne to want to speak with her.

"You have the right to know about this before anyone else does," says Anne. "It's completely up to you what you do with this information, but I feel it's only right that I tell you in person."

"Can't you just tell me now?" Brittany is a little annoyed by this.

"It would really be best if it's in person. I'm sorry, but I want to be face to face with you. I feel it's only right."

Brittany is a little annoyed that Anne can't just tell her what she has to tell her over the phone. But she doesn't want to push this woman's buttons. She's got information on what happened, information that may give Brittany the answers she has been hopelessly searching for since that fateful night. She can't blow this opportunity.

"I'm supposed to be going on a trip this weekend," Brittany says, thinking a mile a minute. "But I can come to your place first. I don't care; I can even cancel the trip if I have to. Do you still live at the same house though?"

"Yes, I do," says Anne.

"Well, how's tomorrow afternoon?"

"That's fine with me. And will you do me a huge favor and keep quiet about us meeting? At least until afterward?"

This is a little paranoid, Brittany feels, although she can

understand why Anne wouldn't want the press to find out. She remembers all the phone calls, the news reporters asking for interviews. Sometimes, reporters would find her when she was out running errands with her grandparents. The three of them would be heading to their car, and suddenly several microphones would be shoved into their faces. "How are you coping?" the reporters would ask. "How does it feel to know that your mother's killer is still at large?" Brittany was tempted to respond to their questions with a question of her own: *How does it feel to know that you have nothing better to do with your pathetic lives than to fuck people over?* But she never asked them this. She didn't want to upset her grandparents more than they already were by all of the commotion that served as an explicit reminder of the turmoil they were in.

So Brittany understands why Anne wants her to keep quiet about them meeting. That, along with the fact that she doesn't want anyone bothering *her* about it, is why she tells Anne that she'll keep it between the two of them.

chapter 7

It's nearly 8:00 in the evening as Brittany sits in the Stevenson Dining Hall eating a late dinner with the five friends with whom she will be going on the spring break trip.

"She really misses me," says Brittany. "I feel like I owe her a visit, you know? And it's really not that far out of the way. I mean, I could probably still get to your house by tomorrow night." Brittany is addressing Jennifer, who is seated directly across from her. On one side of Jennifer is her boyfriend Nick, who has his arm around her. On the other side of Jennifer is Jeff, Kyle's boyfriend. Kyle is seated next to Jeff. And on the other side of the table, sitting next to Brittany, is Amanda. It is nice how this dining hall has long tables for a large group of friends like themselves to sit at. It beats having to push tables together any day.

"Don't worry about it," says Jennifer. "We'll still have the whole week to hang out."

"Thanks for understanding," says Brittany, taking a bite of her salad. This is going smoothly enough. She knows that she can get to this little rendezvous the following afternoon without any of her friends knowing what is really going on. She wants nothing more than to leave them out of this mess.

"Shouldn't I still go with you though?" suggests Amanda. "I mean, I was going to go with you originally since I don't have a car on campus."

Or maybe this won't go so smoothly. "No, it's fine," Brittany says. "I know how to get there since it's only about a half hour from where my grandparents live. And then I can just use my GPS to get to your place." She looks over at Jennifer.

"And besides," Brittany laughs, "it would probably be really boring for any of you guys to have to visit my old neighbor with me."

"Well," says Kyle. "I still think someone should probably go with you. Because you have, like, no idea how to get up to Jennifer's. I mean, what if you get lost or something?"

How is Brittany going to get out of this now? Will Anne tell her anything if she has a friend with her? She could always wait until summer to visit, but in the meantime, she would be consumed with curiosity, which would trigger the painful memories that are associated with her past. She wants get this over with. She can't stand to have to wait.

"Yeah," says Jennifer. "Now that I think about it, someone probably should go with you. I mean, you've never been up to my house before, and there aren't exactly a lot of places to ask for directions way up in the Appalachian Mountains."

"You got that right," says Kyle. "It's a good thing Jennifer's parents knew where they were going or we would've been fucked."

"It's okay, though." Brittany is beginning to get frustrated with her friends even though she knows that they are just looking out for her. This is none of any of their businesses and she doesn't want to bring them down by making it their businesses. "I mean, I can just risk it because it's not fair to you guys. And I've obviously got my phone so I can call you, Jennifer, if I get lost or something."

"Brittany, why won't you just let me go with you?" Amanda asks her. "Like, it's seriously stupid to go up there all by yourself when you've never even been there before. And I honestly don't care, because like you said, we'd still be getting to Jennifer's by tomorrow night."

Brittany knows there is no way out of this now unless she cancels the trip altogether, which is not something she wants to do. Not only will it make all of her friends suspicious, but she has been looking forward to this trip for so long and she knows she is going to need it after the turmoil she will be putting herself through tomorrow.

Amanda will be going with her. This means she will have to tell her everything. It's better, though, than telling all five of her friends right then and there and betraying Anne's trust five times over. Not to mention the huge damper she'd be putting on the trip by revealing this personal situation that she'd much rather just keep personal.

But now she is going to have to drag Amanda along for the hell ride, and this is not something she has ever intended on putting any of her friends through. It sucks. She can't win.

"Well, I don't think my neighbor's going to like that I'm bringing someone who she hasn't met before," she says. She knows that any further arguing is useless, but at least she can say she tried.

"You can just tell her that you're going on a trip and you don't want to have to drive alone," says Jeff, whom Brittany hasn't heard a word out of since they sat down for dinner. Jeff's the quiet type, but he's cool. He's good for Kyle.

"Yeah," says Brittany, feeling defeated. She wonders if Jeff would have said the same thing if he knew the real reason why she is visiting Anne. Probably not. He'd probably respect her decision to go alone.

"So it's settled then," says Kyle, setting down his soda. "Brittany and Amanda are going together and then the rest of us are going in Nick's car. Just like we planned." He smiles.

"Sounds like fun," says Nick, rolling his eyes. Brittany notices Jennifer slap him in the ribs under the table, probably hoping that Kyle didn't pick up on his sarcasm. She suspects that Nick isn't too thrilled with the idea that Jennifer's ex-boyfriend, gay or not, is going to be spending the next week with them. But Jennifer and Kyle will always be close friends. They're two peas in a pod. The sooner Nick accepts that fact, the better.

It's nearly midnight as Brittany lies in her bed under the covers, trying to fall asleep. She is all alone because her roommate has already headed home for break. She's never been real close to her roommate either. The girl is quite the bitch when it all comes down to it. But maybe she feels the same way about Brittany. Maybe that's how roommates are supposed to feel about each other, at least in small college dorm rooms like this one. It's as though it would be crossing some sort of line for them to be close. It's as though they should keep their distances from one another based on the fact that they live together.

She is not at all tired. She has far too much on her mind that doesn't even have anything to do with the roommate. First, she has to finish getting her things together in the morning. Then, of course, she has a six-hour drive, and sometime during that long drive she will have to tell Amanda the real reason why she is visiting her old neighbor. And how is this whole thing with Anne going to turn out, seeing that Amanda is there? Perhaps she can find a way to persuade Anne that Amanda will keep quiet. And hopefully Amanda *will* keep her mouth shut.

But more important than how Anne will react to Amanda's presence is what it is she has to say. What in the world does Anne know about what happened to her and her mother? Why can't Anne have just told her everything over the phone? Brittany figures that Anne is just one of those people who feel that some things aren't suitable to discuss unless they are done in person. This means that whatever she has to say is serious.

All of this wondering brings back the memories of that night. God, what a nightmare it had been for her. Hell on Earth. The one thing that stands out from that night the most for her is the image of her mother lying dead on the bathroom floor in a pool of her own blood. That image will be with Brittany as long as she lives.

Why me? Brittany wonders. *Why did all of this have to happen to me?* None of her friends have ever experienced the hell she's been through. This makes her envy them and pity herself.

Lying in the dark of her room, where no one is around to see her, Brittany begins to cry silently, allowing the tears to run down her face and onto the pillow.

THE FOLLOWING MORNING AROUND EIGHT a.m., Brittany hears a knocking at her door. "Brittany, are you in there?" she hears Amanda calling out to her. "I thought we were supposed to meet outside."

"Shit," Brittany whispers to herself. She is sitting on the bathroom toilet seat inside her dorm room. She was just in the process of cutting her wrist, and now the blood is beginning to seep out. She quickly sucks the blood up, hoping there will be no more of it. As she gets up off the toilet seat to wash the razor blade off in the sink, she is pissed at herself for having lost track of the time. She hasn't even finished packing. And how in the hell is she going to make this work with Amanda still not knowing what is *really* going on?

As she opens the bathroom door, she hears Amanda knocking again. "I'm coming," she shouts. She quickly rushes to her suitcase sitting on her bed. She opens it up and puts the razor blade inside of the makeup bag that she has stowed away inside of the suitcase. She is relieved to see that she is no longer bleeding. She didn't have a chance to cut that far in this time. Not that she ever has. She always freaks out that she's going to hit a vein. Usually a little blood comes out, she feels what little relief she needs to get her through the day, and then she is done.

She rushes to the door, unlocks it, and opens it. "Come on in," she tells Amanda.

"Did you oversleep?" Amanda asks her as she enters the room, shutting the door behind her.

"No, I just lost track of time," says Brittany, heading back over to her suitcase to stuff the clothes she has laid out on the bed inside of it.

"Is everything okay?" asks Amanda.

"Yeah, I'm fine," says Brittany as she heads over to her drawer across from the bed to grab something to wear for today.

"Are you sure?"

"Amanda, I'm fine." Brittany is now getting a little frustrated with her friend as she heads back over to the bed to zip up her suitcase. She needs to go into the bathroom to change into her clothes for the day. As she zips up the suitcase, she notices that she is bleeding again. "Shit," she says, sucking up the blood.

"Brittany, you know you can tell me if something's wrong," says Amanda, sitting down on the side of the bed beside Brittany's suitcase.

She's not giving up, is she? Brittany thinks to herself. She takes a deep breath before sitting down on the bed as well, the suitcase separating her from Amanda. She is a little annoyed by this, so she picks it up and sets it down on the floor. For a moment afterward, neither of them says anything, and from this silence, Brittany realizes that it's time to tell Amanda the truth.

"I haven't exactly been honest with you," she says.

"What do you mean?" asks Amanda.

"About why I'm visiting this neighbor of mine."

Amanda allows her to go on.

"You know about everything that happened when I was fourteen, right?"

Amanda nods. Of course she knows. How could she forget that night last year when they'd had a sleepover in Amanda's dorm? It was the weekend, and Amanda's roommate was at home visiting her family. They'd gotten drunk on booze Brittany had purchased from an upperclassman, and because of this, Brittany felt comfortable enough opening up to Amanda about her past. At first, it seemed to Brittany that Amanda didn't believe a word of it. But then, when Brittany began to cry, she could tell by Amanda's change of facial expression that she knew that Brittany was serious.

"Well, my neighbor knows something about it," Brittany continues. "I don't know what, but I wanted to find out. But now, I don't know if I can handle it." Brittany's eyes begin to fill with tears, but she forces herself not to cry.

"It just reminds me of everything. I just want to forget about it, you know? Pretend it never happened. But then there's another part of me that wants justice for my mom.

"The last time I spoke to her, she told me she loved me." The tears come to her eyes again, and this time it's an even bigger struggle to hold them back. "But I didn't say it back. I didn't think it was that important." She knows that there is no use now in preventing the tears. They are going to come.

"I'm so scared without her," she goes on. A tear escapes her eye and runs down her cheek, but she doesn't bother wiping it away. "It's really, really scary to think that I'll never see her again, even after I die. I want to see her again really badly. I miss her so much. I miss my mom so much." She now lets it all out, bursting into sobs. She allows herself to fall into Amanda's open arms.

"Brittany, I'm so sorry," Amanda says to her. She sounds like she might cry too. "Why didn't you tell me any of this last night at dinner?"

Brittany sits back up and wipes the tears from her eyes, sniffling. "I didn't want anyone to know but me. But then you insisted on coming." She wonders if Amanda is mad now that she knows what she's gotten herself into. "I'm sorry. I didn't want any of the other guys to know."

"It's fine," says Amanda. "I'm just sorry you have to go through all of this. I mean, what did you ever do to deserve this kind of shit?"

"That's what I've always wondered," says Brittany, sniffling again. "I have to do this, though. I have to be strong."

"Are you sure?" asks Amanda.

"Yes," says Brittany. Her eyes are burning from all the tears, but she feels better now. While she didn't want to break down in front of Amanda like this, she has finally allowed herself to let some of the frustration out, the frustration she'd been bottling up for quite some time now. Being vulnerable like this is embarrassing to her; she feels completely exposed, naked. But at the same time, she needs the relief that has come from opening up to someone. It has given her the renewed strength she needs to get through this day.

"I need to do what I can. For my mom."

chapter 8

B rittany knows that she hasn't fully prepared herself for the amount of driving she will be doing today. It's a good six hours from the college to her grandparents' home in Pennsylvania. It will probably take a little longer to get to her old neighborhood in Harrisburg, what with it being the weekend and the possibility of traffic being greater than it would be any other time of the week. But at least she knows where she is going. And she's got a very understanding friend who will be with her along the way.

Once Brittany has grabbed some breakfast in the dining hall, they set off on the road just before 8:45 a.m. Amanda asks her if it's okay if she rests a little since Brittany knows where she is going. Of course Brittany is okay with this. If anything, it's a blessing that she won't have to be talking with anyone on the ride there, at least not the whole way. She really isn't in the mood to talk with anyone. She needs time to herself to think. But she is glad to have the company regardless. She is glad she isn't alone in all of this, that if she feels on the verge of having a panic attack, there will be someone with her to help calm her down.

The drive is relaxing at first, as it always has been when she's headed to and from college in her grandparents' old car, which they gave her the previous year as an early nineteenth birthday present just before her spring semester began. But, as long a drive as it is, it begins to become tedious after the first few hours. Brittany decides, since her tank is running close to empty, that they'll stop for gas. It'll give her a chance to stretch her limbs and ready herself for the long stretch of road she still has ahead of her.

As they pull up at the pump and Brittany shuts off the ignition, Amanda wakes up. She looks over at the clock as Brittany gets out of the car and realizes she's been asleep for the last couple of hours. She's surprised she was able to even fall asleep, having her head leaned up against the window like she did. She feels a little guilty and irresponsible, like she should have stayed awake to help Brittany if she needed it. Brittany told her she knew how to get where they were going, but still.

"Sorry I fell asleep like that," Amanda says to Brittany as she gets out of the car to stretch and feels the fresh air move through her.

"It's fine," Brittany tells her as she pumps the gas. "Don't worry about it."

"Well, I won't sleep anymore." Amanda laughs and takes a look around at their surroundings. It sounds like they've just gotten off of the freeway. She can hear cars zooming by in the distance.

This area isn't the least bit familiar to her. She's never driven around Ohio or Pennsylvania before. Being from Florida, she's flown to and from school every semester. This reminds her, too, that her parents were expecting her to fly back home for break and she hasn't talked with them in a few days. They weren't all that happy to hear she wouldn't be coming home, but they have to realize that this kind of an opportunity just isn't worth passing up. Spending time with her closest friends in a beautiful home in the isolation of the mountains is quite honestly like a dream come true for her.

Hopefully, though, this situation with Brittany won't ruin things. She feels selfish hoping this, but she just wants everything to work out smoothly so that they can all just have a good time. The situation is odd too. Does the neighbor want to give Brittany dirt on her mother's killer? If so, why wouldn't she have just gone to the police about it? Does she want to leave it up to Brittany or something? It sounds a little fishy to her, but she cares about Brittany enough to do what she can to help her through this. She just hopes this isn't a waste.

Once Brittany is done filling up the tank, she and Amanda use the restroom before getting back onto the road. They don't talk much for the next four hours. They spend most of the time listening to music and enjoying the exhilarating feeling of the fresh air rushing past them. It's warm for early April, and the sun shines bright as ever in the clear blue sky. If Brittany didn't already know what she was in for, she may have found herself misled by this weather. She's glad, though, that it's nice out. It helps shallow out the pit of darkness she feels growing inside of her. It gives her the balance she needs to maintain her sanity.

By the time they reach Harrisburg, Brittany is exhausted from the drive. Her ass is numb from sitting in one position for so long, and her right leg has been trying to fall asleep for the past hour. It's gotten to the point where she considered asking Amanda to drive the rest of the way, but she decided against it, knowing that she's already put enough on her friend for one day. And there's more still to come.

She knows they'd better get something to eat before they go to Anne's. She is going to need the energy to deal with whatever it is that is going to be revealed to her.

Shortly after getting off of the freeway, they see a diner up the road. Brittany can see that the town has been built up a little since she was here last, way back when.

"We should probably get something to eat," she tells Amanda as they head further down the road toward the diner. "I don't know if Anne's going have anything for us, and I just want to be prepared, you know?"

"No, I agree with you completely," says Amanda. "I'm getting really hungry myself."

"Are you okay with going to this diner?" Brittany asks, hoping for a quick response before she has to pass the place.

"Yeah, sure," says Amanda. "Hopefully there will be some stuff for us to eat."

"Yeah, I know," says Brittany, getting into the turning lane just in time. There aren't many places that have a whole lot of food for vegetarians, at least not around here as far as Brittany can remember. But the diner's probably a better bet than any of the nearby fast-food restaurants.

"Oh, I just realized," says Amanda as they pull into the parking lot. "You never said her name until just now."

"Oh, wow," says Brittany, forcing a laugh as she pulls into a parking spot. It's not too crowded here for a Saturday. Then again, it is almost three in the afternoon. It's past lunch, but it isn't quite time for dinner.

She thinks about what Amanda has just said as she shuts off the ignition. She's a little surprised that she's been so discreet as to not even give her friend the name of the person they will be visiting. It reminds her how much of a wall she has built up around her. She really does keep to herself more than she often realizes.

"What time are we supposed to see her anyway?" asks Amanda, unbuckling her seatbelt.

"I just told her the afternoon," says Brittany. "I guess I should have been a little more specific. She's probably waiting for us." Waiting for *her*, rather. She begins to feel herself growing concerned again over how Anne will react to Amanda's presence.

"Well, let's eat then," says Amanda, opening her door and stepping out of the car. Brittany takes her keys out of the ignition and follows suit, locking up once the doors have been shut.

Upon entering the restaurant, they are greeted by a hostess, whom Brittany instantly recognizes as her old friend Claire. *So much for not running into people*, she thinks to herself. But at the same time, she can't help but feel a little good about this.

"Is it just the two of you?" asks Claire, grabbing two menus to walk Brittany and Amanda to their table.

"Claire?" says Brittany. She's surprised that her friend doesn't recognize her. Has she really changed *that* much since they were fourteen?

Claire takes a better look at her. "Oh my God! Brittany!" She rushes over to hug Brittany. "It's been such a long time."

"I know," says Brittany. She can feel her spirits being inevitably lifted. She never realized how good it would make her feel to see Claire again like this. She needs this right now, as overwhelming as the mixture of the day's emotions may be.

"I'm so sorry I didn't stay in touch with you after what happened," Claire says as they finish hugging.

"It's not your fault I had to change schools," says Brittany.

"So why are you here?" asks Claire. "I mean, I'm glad you're here."

Brittany laughs. *Yeah, exactly,* she thinks. *What the hell am I doing in a town where my mother was murdered? Why would I ever want to come back here?* "Well," she says, "me and my friend Amanda—oh," she interrupts herself, realizing she hasn't yet introduced her friends to one another. "Amanda, this is Claire. Claire, Amanda."

"Nice to meet you," Amanda and Claire say to one another as they shake hands.

"So," continues Brittany from where she left off in her explanation to Claire, which she is going to have to lie about, "Amanda and I are getting ready—"

"Here, let me take you guys to your table." interrupts Claire, looking behind them. Brittany turns to see an old couple coming in.

"I'll be right with you," she tells the couple.

"But go on," she tells Brittany. "I'm listening." She turns to walk them to their table.

Brittany figures it isn't going to be that hard to lie to Claire since she's already sidetracked with work as it is. "We're heading up to a friend's house," she says, "and I figured we'd just visit my old town since it's on the way. It might give me some closure on the whole thing." Closure? Wow. She forgot how good she can be at improvising.

"That's really good," says Claire, setting the menus down on a table in a center booth. "I wish I wasn't working right now. We could talk a little bit."

"It's okay," says Brittany as she and Amanda sit down on either side of the table. "I understand."

"Well, let me at least give you my number. How long are you going to be here?"

"Well," says Brittany, "we're actually heading up to our friends' house tonight probably."

"Oh," says Claire. Brittany can see the disappointment in her face. "Well, here." She pulls a pen out of her pocket and grabs a napkin off of the table. She jots down her number and then slides it over to Brittany. "If you're ever in town again, just call me, okay? Or you could always just call me anyway."

"Yeah, I can do that," says Brittany, taking the napkin. She is grateful for Claire's kind intentions. It makes her feel a little guilty that she isn't able to find it within herself to meet Claire's enthusiasm.

"Well," Claire says, "I've got to get back to work. It was really nice seeing you again, Brittany."

"You too," Brittany tells her, realizing that there really is no point in trying to get back in touch with Claire. It's a little depressing when she thinks about how people just drift apart as their lives play out.

"It was nice meeting you," Claire tells Amanda.

"Nice meeting you too," says Amanda as Claire turns to head back up to the front of the restaurant to take care of the couple and another group of people who have just walked in.

"She seems really nice," says Amanda.

"Yeah," says Brittany. "We were really close before everything happened."

"It's a shame that you guys couldn't have still been friends," says Amanda.

"Yeah, but I mean, once I moved in with my grandparents, we lived like forty-five minutes away from each other. So it was hard to hang out. And half the time, I didn't want to be around anybody anyway."

Their conversation is interrupted as a middle-aged waitress, whom Brittany does *not* recognize, approaches the table. "Hi, my name is Kathy," she says to them, "and I'll be your server this afternoon. Can I start you ladies out with anything to drink?"

"I'll just have water," says Amanda.

"Okay," says the waitress. She turns to Brittany. "And what would you like?"

"Umm," Brittany says hesitantly, "I'll just have a Coke."

"All right," says the waitress. "I'll be back with them in just a bit."

As the waitress heads toward the back of the restaurant, Amanda gets up out of her seat. "I'm going to use the bathroom," she says.

"Okay," says Brittany. "Do you know where it is?"

"No, but I'll find it."

As Amanda heads over to a young waiter walking by to ask him where the restrooms are, Brittany opens the menu. She hopes there are some suitable vegetarian options at this place. She doesn't want to have to settle for a garden salad. She's got a lot going on right now, and she hasn't had anything substantial to eat since breakfast. She could use some serious protein in her body right now. A veggie burger would do the trick. She turns to the entrée page in hopes that she will see some sort of veggie burger as an option, and lo and behold, there is one. She closes the menu, deciding that that is what she will get.

Setting the menu back down on the table, she wonders if she should give Anne a call to let her know that she will be there soon. Maybe Anne has called her to see if she's coming. She should check.

HE PULLS INTO THE DINER with his wife and daughter. It's been a long time since he's had the chance to take his family out to lunch. He's always so caught up with his job. As though endless paperwork in a tiny office cubicle in a twenty-four-story building should come before spending quality time with his family, but he's got to have a way to pay the bills. At least his boss has let him off the hook this weekend. He doesn't even have any home office work to deal with.

"Let's eat," says his wife as she unbuckles her seatbelt and opens her door. He and his daughter in the backseat follow suit. Once they're all out and all the doors are shut, he locks up and they head up the parking lot to the entrance.

"It's a nice day out," he says, squinting as the sun shines down on them. He looks beside him at his wife and daughter, holding hands with one another. They are both so beautiful. Keira, his daughter, has gotten so tall over the past year. She's ten now and is only a head and a neck shorter than her mother. Her long, curly hair glistens in the sunlight.

"It sure is," says Donna, his wife.

Once they're at the entrance, Russell opens the door and holds it open for them.

"Why, thank you," says his wife.

Once Donna and Keira have gotten into the restaurant, he notices two young women approaching the entrance, about to leave. He might as well maintain his gentlemanly demeanor and hold the door open for the two of them as well.

"Thank you," says the first girl, who has long, dirty-blonde, curly hair just like his daughter's.

"You're welcome," he says as the second girl comes out.

"Thanks." She smiles at him.

"Sure thing." And then it hits him. Her green eyes, her beautiful facial features, her straight, dirty-blonde, shoulder-length hair. He knows who this girl is. It's been almost six years, but she hasn't changed enough for him to not recognize her. He is fully certain that the girl he has just held the door for is none other than Brittany Taylor.

She's come back. She's come back for him.

As he enters the restaurant, he does everything he can not to fall into a panic, a continuation of the panic he felt that night when she got away from him and ran screaming down the street. He'd fucked up, and now his fuckup has come back to haunt him.

"Three?" the hostess at the podium asks them.

"Yes, three," says Donna.

As the hostess grabs three menus and turns to lead them to their table, he knows he needs to think fast. He can't just sit in this restaurant and have lunch with his wife and daughter and pretend that everything is okay. It sure as hell isn't okay, and he needs to do something about it before it is too late.

While they walk to their table, he reaches into his pocket for his cell phone.

"Hello?" he says into the receiver.

Donna and Keira, who are about to sit down in a booth, turn to look at him.

Work. He's gotten called in for work. That's what he'll make it sound like.

"You need me?" he says to no one. "Well, I'm about to have

lunch with my wife and daughter ... okay ..." He lets out a sigh of disappointment. "Okay." He clicks the end button and puts the phone back in his pocket.

"What was that about?" Donna asks him.

"I just got called in for a conference. In DC."

"Are you serious?" He can tell that Donna is frustrated. She hates the lack of family time just as much as he does. They were finally getting the chance to spend some time together today, and now it's ruined.

"Yeah, I really can't get out of it this time."

"You're not even on call, though."

"I know, but I've got to do this. I'm really sorry. I will explain everything as soon as I get more details."

"Well, you can at least take us home." Donna stands up in the booth, prompting Keira to stand as well.

"No," he says. "You guys stay. We've been planning to do this for weeks. And you're already here, so you might as well just get something to eat." He reaches into his back pocket for his wallet. "I'll give you girls money for a cab."

"You're missing the point," Donna is really getting irritated now. He's got to find a way to calm her down, to get her to work with him. "This day was about us all being together."

"And I promise we'll get another day like this. Just not today. Please. I'll talk to my boss about no more late notices."

Donna hesitates for a moment, but to his relief, she sits back down and Keira does the same. Opening his wallet, he pulls out four twenties—two for lunch and two for a cab—and hands them over to Donna. He then bends down and kisses Keira on the forehead. "Daddy promises he'll be around more in the future."

He can tell by the look of disappointment on her face that

she isn't buying it. Why should she? He can't count the number of broken promises he's made her. But he has no choice right now. He needs to prepare himself for what is happening.

Saying his final good-byes to them, he heads back out of the diner.

chapter 9

About ten minutes after leaving the diner, Brittany and Amanda pull up into Anne's driveway and Brittany shuts the car off.

"I guess we should get out now," she says to Amanda. The anticipation is killing her.

"Are you ready for this?" Amanda asks her.

"I don't know." Brittany has no idea what is so important that Anne has to tell *her* instead of just going to the police about it, but she is appreciative of it. "Let's just go."

As they get out of the car, Brittany can't help but focus on the house across the street, the house that was once her home. It isn't the abandoned shack that the horror movies claim it would be, like Michael Myers's home in the *Halloween* franchise. Instead, it is in just as good of a condition as it was when she lived there. It hasn't changed much. The shutters are a different color, and there is an array of flowers in the yard, an array that her mother and she would never have made the time to create and tend to. These are the only differences she can make out. Other than these, it's completely and disturbingly the same.

"Was that your house?" Amanda asks her.

"Yeah," says Brittany, regaining her focus on the here and now. "Sorry. I kind of—"

"Its fine," says Amanda.

They shut their doors, and Brittany locks up. They then walk together down the cement pathway to Anne's front door. Every step Brittany takes allows the butterflies in her stomach to surge through her more and more, to the point where she knows there is nothing left for her to do but embrace her nerves. She's here and she has to do this. Whatever is to come will come.

When they reach the front door, Brittany takes a deep breath before ringing the doorbell.

Moments later, she hears footsteps inside the house. She then sees a woman peering out one of the sidelights to see who it is. She hears the door unlock before seeing it open.

"Hi," says Brittany the second she sees Anne. She can see that Anne has aged a bit since they last saw one another those years back. Her short hair is graying, and wrinkles have begun to emerge on her face. She's still a pretty woman, though.

"My goodness," says Anne, "you look so much more grown up than when I last saw you." She stares Brittany up and down and then turns to Amanda.

Brittany forces a smile. "I hope it's okay that I brought my friend," she says. "We're going on a trip, and she insisted on driving with me so I wouldn't have to go alone." She hopes her excuse will prove to Anne that there was nothing she could have done about it.

Anne glances at Amanda. It looks to Brittany that she isn't the least bit happy to see her friend. This is what she was worried about. Now what?

"I-I can wait in the car," Amanda offers awkwardly.

"No, that isn't necessary," Anne says to her hesitantly. "It's good to see Brittany has a caring friend. But you have to promise that you're going to keep this to yourself."

"Yeah, that's not a problem," Amanda agrees. "It's up to Brittany who knows and who doesn't know."

"Well, all right then," says Anne. "Why don't you both come on in?" She moves aside, allowing room for the two of them to enter.

"I promise you Amanda's the only person who knows why I'm here," says Brittany, stepping into the house.

"Well, that's good," says Anne, shutting the front door once Amanda has come in. "Can I get either of you anything to drink? I just made some tea."

"Tea's fine," says Brittany.

"Is tea okay with you?" Anne asks Amanda.

"Yes," says Amanda. "Thank you."

"All right," says Anne. "Well, why don't you two have a seat while I'm getting the drinks?" Anne points to the sofas in the adjoining family room to their right. "And I'll be right in." She heads off into what looks to them like the kitchen area.

Brittany and Amanda take a seat next to one another on the nearest sofa. Brittany notices that the furniture is mostly shades of light pink, aside from the glass table in the center of the two sofas and the wooden rocking chair beside the sofa they are sitting on.

Brittany wonders if Anne lives alone here. If she remembers correctly from what her mother had told her, Anne was divorced. It seems that she's never remarried. She's sure Anne would have told her if she had a husband coming home.

Anne returns, carrying a tray with three empty glasses and a pitcher filled with iced tea. "Here we are," she says, setting the tray down on the glass table. She takes a seat in the wooden rocking chair, allowing her to reach the glasses to fill them with tea.

"So," says Anne, pouring the first glass of tea and handing it to Brittany, who hands it over to Amanda, "we're all aware that you didn't come here to engage in small talk with your old neighbor." She pours the second glass of tea and hands it over to Brittany.

"Umm ..." says Brittany, not knowing how exactly to respond as she takes the glass of tea.

"I mean, let's be honest," says Anne, pouring the final glass of tea for herself and then setting down the pitcher. She settles herself in her chair, sips her tea before setting it down on the side table next to her, and looks over at Brittany. "We barely knew one another."

Haven't we been through this on the phone? Brittany thinks to herself.

"This isn't going to be an easy matter to discuss, Brittany," she says. "I'll do the best I can to be sensitive about it." She pauses to take a deep breath. "How do you begin something like this?"

"Well, what is it you want to tell me?" offers Brittany, setting her glass of tea down on the table so she doesn't have to hold it. She really isn't thirsty after the two Cokes she just drank at the restaurant.

"There are a lot of things that I've wanted to tell you, but I've simply been too cowardly to do so."

"It's okay," says Brittany impatiently, hoping that Anne will just cut to the chase. "Just tell me. That's why I'm here."

Anne takes a moment to respond. "This isn't easy for me, Brittany," she says.

"So please just be patient with me."

"Okay," says Brittany. "Take your time." She is being half sarcastic, but she also feels a little for Anne. This is a brave thing for her to be doing.

Anne takes another deep breath. "I won't be surprised if this ends with you being angry at me. After all, I only waited almost six years to tell you this."

"Wait, so you didn't just find out about this?" Brittany is incredulous.

"Only a part of it," says Anne.

"What do you mean 'only a part of it'?"

"Brittany, just let her talk," says Amanda, intervening.

Taking the advice of her friend, Brittany calms down, allowing Anne to continue.

"It was hours before it all happened," Anne begins. "I was coming out to get my mail and I saw a man standing on the sidewalk across the street. He was looking up at you in your bedroom. I caught glimpses of you. You looked like you were dancing around. That's how I knew he wasn't just looking at your house as he claimed."

Brittany remembers the dance routine she'd been forming to the song "Walk Away." It's weird for her to think that while she was dancing around and having a good time, all of this was happening right around her. How could she have been so unaware?

"So," Anne continues, "I asked him what the trouble was. I startled him, which was a sure sign. As I said, he claimed he was just admiring your house, but I think he knew I was onto him."

Brittany can see that Anne looks like she is about to cry.

"I thought since I'd caught him that that was the end," she

says tearfully. "I didn't think that anything would happen. I thought he would have been intelligent enough to know that if he did anything, I'd be able to point him out to the police. But then, after that night, I thought about it more." Her eyes fill with tears. "I knew nothing about this man. I didn't know his name. I didn't know where he lived. For all I knew, he could have been from another state."

"Couldn't you have at least given the police a description?" asks Brittany.

Anne considers this for a moment. "I was scared," she says. "If my seeing him hadn't stopped him from doing what he wanted to do, then who's to say the police could have stopped him from coming after me once I'd tried to identify him?"

Brittany is beginning to wonder what the point is of her even being here right now. Is this just so Anne can ease her guilt?

"I was also ashamed," says Anne, her eyes filling with tears again. "You don't know how much guilt I've had since then."

Brittany was right. This is all about Anne and her guilt.

"To know you could have prevented a murder but didn't," Anne continues. A tear runs down her cheek. She quickly wipes it away.

This is just too pathetic for Brittany to bear. "Well," she says to Anne, "maybe if you'd helped the police find this son of a bitch like you should have, you wouldn't be feeling so guilty right now."

"Brittany," says Amanda, putting her hand on Brittany's shoulder.

"No!" says Brittany, turning to Amanda. She points at Anne. "She could have helped find him, but she didn't. And now he's still out there doing God knows what to other people."

"If you'd please just let me finish," pleads Anne.

"Oh, there's more?" Brittany is enraged. "What, now you want to apologize to me and hope we can be friends or some shit? Well, fuck that! I drove six hours here today, hoping that I could get something out of this. But I can see that isn't going to happen."

"Please," Anne begs.

Is this woman serious? Brittany forces herself to calm down. She can't wait to see how much more pathetic this woman is about to get.

"Yes, I was a coward," says Anne. "No argument could prove otherwise. But I didn't have you come here, Brittany, only so that you can leave more frustrated at the world than I'm sure you already are." She pauses. "There is more to it than what I've just told you."

Brittany feels a little guilty now for having been so mean to Anne. Perhaps she shouldn't have been so quick to react, assuming Anne actually *does* know something that can help catch her mother's murderer.

"So may I continue?" asks Anne.

Brittany nods.

Anne sighs. "It was a little less than a month ago," she begins, "and I was in the middle of my shift at the bank. I was with a customer when, out of the corner of my eye, I saw a man come in. At first, I didn't make anything of it. *Just another customer*, I thought. But then, when he went over to my coworker and spoke with her about whatever it was he needed, I recognized his voice. I'd only spoken to him that one time years ago, but somehow, it was enough to remember him by.

"He was about to leave, and since I was done with my customer, I was able to get a good look at him. It was *him* all right. The thing that got to me was that as he was heading out the door he turned and looked right at me. It wasn't a threatening look. It was a look of worry, worry that I'd recognized him.

"When we were closing up, I asked Becky, my coworker, about him. I told her he looked like someone I'd seen before and his name might jog my memory. So she gave it to me." She pauses. "His name is Russell Thompson.

"I obviously didn't ask Becky for anything else, because I didn't want her to get suspicious. So, on my own, I checked the bank's records for a Russell Thompson, and from there I got his information. Here, I have it all written down." She reaches across the table, lifting up a stack of magazines. She pulls a piece of loose-leaf paper out from under the stack and hands it to Brittany.

Brittany takes it from her. She can see that Anne has the name and a phone number and address written down. "I can't believe this is happening," she says. "It almost seems too easy. I mean, I'd think he would have left town and never come back. But he's been here all this time?"

"Well," says Anne, "I doubt he decided to flee and then return years later. But to think he managed to avoid me for nearly six years in a small town like this … He's a smart man. But hopefully, with the information I've given you"—she points to the piece of paper Brittany has in her hands—"the police will be able to catch him."

"Yeah," says Brittany. "We have to go the police about this. And what if they want to talk to you?" She doesn't think that just giving the police this piece of paper will be enough to arrest Russell with. They're going to want to hear the testimony from Anne herself.

"Whatever needs to happen," says Anne.

Brittany turns to Amanda. "We should get going." She gets up off of the sofa.

Amanda stands up with her, setting her nearly empty glass tea down on the tray. "Thanks for doing this," she says to Anne.

"I hope it's enough," says Anne. "Well, let me walk you both to the door." She pulls herself out of her chair and leads Brittany and Amanda out of the family room and into the foyer, where she opens the front door for them. As Amanda says good-bye and steps outside, Anne puts a hand on Brittany's shoulder.

"Brittany," she says.

Brittany turns to her.

"I'm sorry I let you down."

Brittany forces a smile. "Thank you," she says as she steps outside to where Amanda is waiting for her. She hears the door shut behind her.

This is what she has been searching for all along, this immense relief, this freeing of her soul. He got away with what he did, and after all these years, Brittany had come to accept that there was no hope for justice. But now she is seeing that there can in fact be light at the end of the tunnel, even the darkest and longest of tunnels. No matter how bad and hopeless things have felt for her at times, she now knows that things can always get better. There is always the possibility for good.

It's time to finally make this man pay for what he did.

As she and Amanda walk side by side down the pathway to the car, she pulls her phone out of her purse and sees that it's just after four o'clock. The sun is shining as bright as it has all day. Its light shines down on them, forcing them to squint as they talk. So much has happened in the past hour. It is a tremendous amount for Brittany to take in, and there is still more to come with them going to the police. Brittany feels bad that she is putting Amanda through all of this, but Amanda insists that she is happy to be here for her.

They get into the car, and Brittany starts the engine. They back out of the driveway, and as Brittany turns to see if any cars are coming down the road, she glimpses a brown Volkswagen parked at the curb in front of the house next to her old home. Seeing no cars aside from this one, she turns out of the neighborhood, clueless to the fact that in that car sits Russell Thompson.

chapter 10

Russell knows that there isn't much time if he expects to catch up to Brittany and that friend of hers. There is no doubt in his mind that they will be going to the police. That woman just couldn't keep her mouth shut any longer, could she? Not after seeing him in the bank a few weeks ago.

Well, now she is going to pay.

Russell takes his black leather gloves out of his coat pocket and puts them on. He doesn't want to leave any fingerprints. He then opens his car door and steps outside. After shutting the door, he slides his hands into his coat pockets. He doesn't want anyone who might see him getting suspicious as to why he is wearing gloves on a nice spring day like this.

He casually crosses the street and heads up her driveway. He looks up and around, making it look as though he is gazing at the scenery in interest as opposed to what he is really doing, which is looking to see if there is anyone outside who can see him. As far as he can see, there is nobody. This makes it a hell of a lot easier.

Once he's reached the top of her driveway, he turns and

starts down her pathway. He cannot wait to see her reaction when she answers the door. She is definitely going to be in for a surprise.

As he reaches the front door, he takes his right hand out of his pocket and knocks three times.

ANNE IS AT HER KITCHEN sink, washing out the pitcher that the tea had been in, when she hears the knocking. "They must have forgotten something," she says to herself as she sets the pitcher down in the sink and removes her dishwashing gloves, placing them on the edge of the sink. She heads out of the kitchen to answer the door.

As she walks through the living room and reaches the front door, she doesn't bother checking to see who it is. She is sure that it is Brittany and her friend. Who else could it be after such a short period of time?

But as she opens the door, fear comes over her as she sees who it is standing there. *This can't be happening*, she thinks to herself. How could he possibly have known what she'd just been up to?

"What do you want?" she asks him, hearing the shakiness in her voice. She knows full well what his intentions are. He's here to kill her for what she's done.

Anne moves swiftly, pushing against the door to close it and lock it, but she feels the pressure from the other side of the door. To her horror, Russell is trying to force his way in. "Please, leave me alone," she pleads.

Russell pushes harder, knocking her backward as he forces his way in.

"Help!" she screams as Russell kicks the door closed once

he is all the way inside. She has no time to run before he comes at her, wrapping his gloved hands tightly around her neck.

Anne gags, desperate for air. She knows she is going to have to fight with everything she has in her if she expects not to be strangled to death by him.

She uses her arms to try to pry Russell's hands off of her neck, but his grip is far too strong. She should kick at his legs. Maybe she'll hurt him enough so she can free herself.

As she reaches her legs out to kick at him, she accidentally kicks her side table in the adjoining family room, knocking it over. She hears the shattering of the glass lamp that rested on top of it. But she doesn't let this stop her. She kicks at his shins, hoping it will be impacting.

He doesn't budge.

As the seconds pass, Anne feels the horror of knowing that she is going to die. She also begins to feel lightheaded. Everything is becoming blurry, not only because she is being denied oxygen but because her eyes are filling with tears. Her whole body feels like it will explode from the pressure of needed air.

It doesn't take long before she gives up the fight. One second she feels the vagueness of her surroundings, and the next she feels nothing. She is gone.

Russell is pleased to see that she is dead. He is able to tell because her head is tilted to the side and she is no longer twitching. His rush gone, he lets go of her neck, allowing her body to fall to the ground.

He takes a look around. On the floor, he sees the knocked-over table and the shattered lamp. There is also a picture frame that has fallen over. When the police find her body, it's going to look like there was a struggle.

But it doesn't have to appear to be the struggle he knows it was. Not if he can find something in this house to make it look like she committed suicide. An empty bottle of pills would be the best thing. If she has any pills, they'd probably be in her bedroom bathroom in the medicine cabinet. The bathroom's probably just down the hallway.

He knows that before he goes looking for the pills, he should take a look outside to see if anyone happens to be out there looking in. Shit if there are. The anticipation of finding this out sends a rush of adrenaline up his spine as he steps into the living room and moves the curtain aside to peer out the window.

Seeing that there is no one outside, he lets out a deep breath of relief. This woman had shouted a bit. Someone could have easily heard her. He's going to need to find a way of being more careful with the other two.

Turning away from her window, he heads down her foyer to where the bedrooms look to be. It's only a one-story house, so he isn't going to have to look very far.

As he comes upon the first door to his right, he opens it and sees that it is only a bedroom. He doesn't see any doors inside that could lead to a bathroom, so he shuts the door and moves on.

The next door is to his left. He opens it up and sees, through the darkness, that it is in fact a bathroom. He feels for the light switch on the side wall and finds that there are two of them. One must be the fan. He tries the one closest to him and sees that he picked the right one as the light comes on.

The bathroom looks to be hers, as opposed to being the guest bathroom. He can tell that this is the case from the toiletries lining the sink and occupying the bathroom countertop.

There is a large mirror above the sink and countertop, spanning the same length. Oftentimes, he's seen the medicine cabinets to be in this spot, but in this bathroom, it is to his side, on the side wall right next to the doorway, that he can see the medicine cabinet. He opens it up and is overjoyed when he sees several bottles of prescription pills on the middle shelf. He can take his pick.

He takes one of the bottles off the shelf and sees from the label that it is Prozac. Can swallowing a whole bottle of Prozac kill someone? If consumed with alcohol, perhaps, and right now he doesn't have a whole lot of other options. It sounds about right. She was depressed, so she did herself in with her antidepressants and booze. The irony of this is beautiful, despite it being a little clichéd.

The bottle is almost full. He's got to get rid of the pills. They won't be in her system, but will they even bother doing an autopsy on her? She was depressed, for Christ's sake. She hated herself for her cowardice and was afraid of what would come from her telling Brittany what he is sure she told her. So she killed herself.

The best thing to do with these pills, he realizes, is to flush them down the toilet.

Shutting the medicine cabinet, he walks past the sink over to the toilet. He lifts up the seat and lid. Such a lady to put both down.

He twists open the lid to the pills and dumps the pills into the water below. He then flushes them down, putting both the seat and lid back down, just as Anne would do.

Carrying the empty bottle of pills and its lid with him, he heads back to where he came in, shutting off the light before leaving the bathroom and shutting the door behind him.

He walks back down the short hallway, and before returning to the foyer where Anne's body lies, he heads into the kitchen to find the alcohol.

He tries the refrigerator first. Inside, just as he hoped, there is a bottle of wine. He takes it out and shuts the door. Unscrewing the cork, he tosses it into the trash that he finds under the sink beside the refrigerator. Once he's done this, he dumps the wine into the sink. He turns the faucet on to make sure that all of it goes down the drain.

Heading back into the foyer, he stands over her. Her eyes are open. So is her mouth. And as for her neck, the red marks are still there, but there's nothing he can do about this. He's in a desperate situation right now. He can only do so much to try to cover up his tracks. The rest is out of his hands.

The police can't take him away from Donna and Keira. That can't happen. That first time was his last time. He failed at Brittany, and he never tried again.

Until now. But it's different now. He's a better man now. How dare this woman try to ruin that for him? How dare she try to sell him out for what he did so long ago? It was wrong of him and he knows that. That should be enough.

He can't go to jail. What would Donna and Keira do without him there to pay the bills?

Forcing himself to focus solely on the task at hand, he places the empty bottle of wine along with the empty bottle of pills next to her right hand and tosses the lid to the pills over by the knocked-over table.

This is quite the little setup he has created. Flawed, but he still can't help but be a little pleased with himself. He did what he had to do. And now it's done.

"You couldn't have just minded your own business," he

says, bending down and shutting her eyelids. Her eyes wouldn't be open after having taken a nearly full bottle of these pills with wine. Those pills and alcohol would have knocked her out before killing her.

Standing back up, he is satisfied to see that his work is done here. He turns and peers out the sidelight before opening the front door. When he sees that, again, there is no one around, he heads out of the house, good and ready for the next step he needs to take.

They couldn't have gotten far. They wouldn't have gone far. But he still needs to get a move on.

UPON ENTERING THE POLICE STATION, a place Brittany had no trouble finding considering the countless times she was here immediately following her mother's murder, Brittany and Amanda can see that the place is practically empty. This could be because it's a weekend or, more importantly, because there are no crimes that have taken place. But there is still a female cop seated behind the front desk.

As they approach the desk, they see the cop look up at them from the paperwork she was sorting through. "How may I help you?" she asks them.

"Hi," says Brittany. "Is there a detective around? I'd like to report a lead on my mother's murder."

"Okay …" says the cop, stacking her paperwork into a neat pile and setting it aside. "We actually do have a detective here right now. I'll see if he's available." She picks up the phone beside her and dials an extension. "Detective Mowry?"

Detective Mowry. The name doesn't ring a bell for Brittany. Of course, she can't forget it's been over five years. Perhaps the detectives she knew are gone or just aren't working for the day. Hopefully, they'll still have her records on file.

"I have two young women here who would like to see you," says the cop. "They'd like to report a lead on a murder … Okay, are you sure? … All right then. I'll bring them back." She hangs up and gets out of her chair and steps out from behind the desk.

"Follow me," she tells them as she starts down the hallway straight ahead.

This is easy enough, thinks Brittany as she and Amanda follow the cop down the hallway. There are doors on either side of the hallway. Most are closed, but they can see that the last one on the left at the end of the hallway is open. This must be where they are headed.

Surely enough, it is.

"Here we are," says the cop, standing aside and allowing them to enter.

"Hello, ladies." As they step inside, Brittany sees a pudgy man with graying hair who looks to be in either his fifties or sixties sitting behind a desk. "Have a seat," he tells them, motioning at the two seats directly across from his desk.

"Thank you for seeing us on such short notice," Brittany tells him as she and Amanda sit down.

"I was about to leave for the day," he says, "given that it's the weekend, but your situation sounded pretty urgent."

"Well, thank you even more then," Brittany tells him.

"So you'd like to report a lead on a murder." He finishes jotting something down on a piece of paper and sets the pen and paper aside. He looks up at Brittany, giving her his full, undivided attention.

"Yes," says Brittany. "I know who my mother's killer is." She hands the piece of paper Anne gave her over to the detective, who, with a confused look on his face, takes it from her.

The cop glances over what is written on the sheet of loose leaf and grins. "What is this?" he asks.

"It's his information," says Brittany. "His name is Russell Thompson, and it's got his address and phone number on it."

"I see that," says the detective. "But where is the evidence?"

Brittany can see where this is going. Anne is going to have to get involved in this. Fortunately, she said she's okay with doing so.

"I got this information from a woman named Anne Lenin," she tells him. "She was my neighbor before I moved away. She lived across the street from me."

"Okay, well, that's something," says the detective, writing the name down below everything else that is written on the paper. He looks back up at Brittany. "How do you spell her last name?"

"L-E-N-I-N," says Brittany.

"And what is your name?" he asks her.

"I'm Brittany Taylor." Brittany sees him write something else down on the piece of paper, probably her name. He glances up at her as she writes, giving her a double take. He'll probably go home and tell his family who she saw at the station today: Brittany Taylor, the celebrity of Harrisburg.

"How long ago did this happen?"

"What?" asks Brittany, not sure is the cop is referring to the murder or her discussion with Anne.

"Your mother's murder," clarifies the detective. "How long ago did it happen?"

"It was about six years ago," says Brittany, wondering what he is trying to get at.

"Six years ago?" He looks to Brittany as though he might burst out laughing.

"Yes, well, a little less," says Brittany, anticipating what he is going to say next. *It doesn't sound good. It's been too long, hasn't it?*

The detective lets out a sigh of disbelief. "You do realize that this witness identification isn't going to hold up in court, not after all of these years."

"No, I didn't realize that," says Brittany, trying to keep her cool. *How can it not be enough?*

"I'm sorry to say, but it's just too little, too late at this point."

"How can it be 'too little, too late'? She saw him the night he killed my mom, and she recognized him at the bank two weeks ago. She knows what she's talking about."

"That isn't going to cut it in court. Now, if she'd come to us back when it happened, then you'd have a lead."

"If only," says Brittany. "But she didn't. I mean, can't you at least call her and talk to her about it?"

"It's not going to make a difference."

"So, in other words, there's absolutely nothing you can do about this?"

"I'm afraid not."

"So he's just going to stay free then. That piece of paper has everything on it. That's him. That has to be him." Brittany can feel a lump building in her throat.

"The most we can do now is you can give me your number, and if anything comes up, I'll give you a call." He hands Brittany a notepad and pen. "Otherwise, I'm sorry I can't be of any help."

Brittany jots down her phone number and hands the

notebook back to him. "This is such bullshit." She gets up out of the chair to leave, but just before doing so, she turns back to the detective.

"Thanks for nothing," she says to him.

"Brittany, wait!" she hears Amanda calling after her as she storms out of the room and back down the hallway. "Brittany!"

Once they're out of the police station and in the parking lot, Brittany begins to feel ashamed with herself. How stupid she was to think that all she had to do was hand over a piece of paper and boom, Russell is behind bars.

"Brittany," she hears Amanda calling after her again.

"I can't believe I was that fucking naïve," says Brittany as she walks to where the car is parked. "I actually thought I could put this all behind me. But they don't even fucking care, do they?" As she reaches the car, which is right by the handicapped spots given that the parking lot was and still is just about empty, she searches her purse for her keys. She sees Amanda coming up beside her. She's probably going to try to calm her down.

"I'm going to his house," Brittany tells her, retrieving her keys. She presses the unlock button twice, unlocking all the doors. "I'm not going let him get away with what he did." She opens her door to get into the driver's seat.

"Brittany, no!" says Amanda. She put her hand around Brittany's arm to try to hold her back.

"Well, what do you want me to do about it then? You heard him. He isn't going to do shit. It was almost six years ago."

She tugs her arm, trying to free it from Amanda's grasp.

"Yeah, but Brittany, we can't go to his house. That's not the way to solve this."

"Yeah, well, I don't see you coming up with any better ideas." She tugs her arm again, but Amanda fights her.

"Brittany, there's nothing we can do about this right now. All we can do now is just head up to Jennifer's and take some time to relax. Now why don't you let me drive the rest of the way?" suggests Amanda.

"I'm fine." *Will Amanda ever let go of her arm?*

"You're not fine."

"Jesus Christ, Amanda! Just let go of me!"

"I'm sorry." Amanda lets go of Brittany's arm and backs away, giving Brittany the space she obviously needs.

As Brittany sees her friend backing away, looking hurt and offended, the guilt comes on. Brittany feels her anger beginning to turn into tears. She feels the sobs rising to the surface and, bursting into tears, she allows herself to lean against the car and slide down onto the pavement. She is exhausted from all of the day's happenings. She doesn't know how much more of this she can honestly take before she loses it.

"Hey," says Amanda soothingly, kneeling down beside Brittany and placing her hand on her shoulder.

"I just wish none of this ever happened," Brittany sobs. "I wish we'd never even come here. I'm so sorry I dragged you through this shit, Amanda."

"It's fine," says Amanda. Brittany can tell she doesn't really mean it. This has to be causing Amanda a great deal of frustration. She just wanted to be able to enjoy her spring break and get away from the day-to-day bullshit. But Brittany's woes have really screwed things up.

"No, it's not," says Brittany, wiping the tears from her face. "Here you are sitting with your psycho friend during her second breakdown in one day. It's definitely *not* fine."

Amanda laughs. "You're not psycho. You're just going through a lot at once."

"That's for sure." Brittany begins to laugh a little herself.

"So do you want me to drive the rest of the way?" Amanda offers again. "It'll give you some time to rest up."

"Fine," says Brittany, sniffling, as both of them stand back up. She hands Amanda her keys. "Be my guest."

Brittany turns to walk to the other side of the car but pauses for a moment and turns back around. "Amanda."

"What?" asks Amanda, who is about to slide into the driver's seat.

"You have to be the best friend I've ever had."

Amanda blushes. "Thank you." Brittany figures she doesn't know quite how to respond to a compliment like this. Brittany probably wouldn't know how to respond either. But it's worth saying. Amanda deserves to know how great she is as a friend. Brittany would be lost without her.

RUSSELL SITS IN HIS CAR. He can see Brittany and her friend getting into their car at the opposite end of the parking lot, which isn't really all that far from where he is parked. They could spot him easily, if only they knew to look for him.

It is a bold move on his part to be parked in the parking lot of the very police station where someone was just trying to have him arrested. But in order to keep track of Brittany's whereabouts, he needs to remain on her tail.

As soon as he sees them drive out of the parking lot and onto the main road, he starts his car.

chapter 11

Russell has no idea where Brittany and her friend are headed to, but with a full tank of gas in his car and plenty of time to kill, given that he actually isn't due back to work until Monday, he is prepared to go wherever it is that they are unknowingly leading him.

He worries a little that they might suspect him, seeing the same car behind them and wondering if the person in that car is following them. So he tries to keep himself a good couple of hundred feet behind them at all times, even if this causes him to lose sight of their car for a few moments. It's better than being caught and having his plan completely ruined.

Once this is all over, he knows he is going to have to move. Probably to another state. Once the police find Anne's body, they're going to know it's him. Unless they think it was suicide like he did his best to set it up to be.

But then there's going to be Brittany and her friend. It won't take the police long to put two and two together.

He can't let them catch him, though. They've already seen

Anne and gone to the police. It's only a matter of time before it's too late for him.

How is he going to explain all of this to Donna and Keira? Donna is going to want to know why they're moving, if she's even willing to go in the first place. What if she isn't willing? She's got family nearby. She might refuse to leave them. Shit, on what planet would she be willing to just pick up and move to another state at the drop of a hat?

Maybe if he makes it about work. She already hates him working so much, though. Keira too. But if he tells her that this new "work gig" will allow him more home time, maybe then he'll be able to sway them.

He's going to have to actually find a job, of course. But he can worry about that later. Right now, it's all about covering up his tracks.

He should have moved and gotten it over with six years ago when he had the chance. Why didn't he? Why did he stick around? It was only a matter of time before his past came back to haunt him. And now it has. Fuck. It's just that Keira was so young. She was just starting school. She was so happy. So was Donna. He didn't want to ruin things for them.

THE DRIVE IS SCENIC FOR Brittany and Amanda just as the drive from the college to Brittany's hometown had been. The huge trees concealing the road in certain areas indicate that they are getting up into the mountains. Upon driving through the vast wooded areas, Brittany is gladder than she has been all day that Amanda has come with her. Kyle was right. She would be in some serious trouble if she got lost up here, especially if she was all alone.

After about two hours of driving, Brittany begins to see

just how high up in the mountains they really are. She can see, to her left, mountainous terrain stretching several hundred feet below. It gives her a rush of fright to know that they are on the edge of a cliff. But at least there are forests to the right of them to give them an alternative to driving off the cliff in a worst-case scenario. Say, for instance, if it was icy and the car started sliding all over the place.

"God, we're really up here," says Amanda. "This is unbelievable."

As Brittany nods in acknowledgment, she hears the GPS tell them that they are now within hundreds of feet from their destination.

Up ahead, Brittany notices a break in the forest that is made more visible by the mailbox. To think mailmen come up here to deliver mail. "I think that's the turn," she tells Amanda, pointing to the mailbox.

Amanda looks from Brittany to where she is pointing. "Oh, okay," she says, putting the turn signal on as she drives up to the spot.

"This is amazing," she says to Brittany as she turns the car up what Brittany can see to be a long, steep, and rather narrow gravel driveway.

Russell is relieved to have seen them turn up perhaps another road. He knows it can't be much further until the two of them have reached their destination. He slowly drives his car up the road to the spot where they just turned. When he reaches the point, he puts his foot on the brake and gazes up what appears to be a gravel driveway. He can't see their car, but he knows they couldn't have gotten far.

And he thought he was going to have to be extra careful when going about doing this. This is the middle of nowhere. No one is going to hear their screams. Could this possibly be any better?

He reaches over to the glove compartment and opens it. He gazes at the semiautomatic pistol hidden inside. *Oh, this is going to be great,* he fantasizes to himself. He might not want to be in this situation, but it is giving him the perfect excuse to fulfill the desires he's been suppressing for so long. He could have continued suppressing his urges for the rest of his life, but now he doesn't have to. He has no choice now but to indulge in them. He got a sampling with Anne. And it felt great.

Shutting the glove compartment, he puts his foot back on the gas and drives off into the sunset. He'll be back later.

"Oh my God," says Brittany once she and Amanda have reached the top of the gravel driveway. "This place is huge." She stares up at the house from in the car. The pictures didn't do it justice. Actually being here right in front of the house is so much different, so much more effective.

The two-story house is very wide, to say the least. The front door, which is uniquely further to the right of the house as opposed to it being dead center, stands below a second story that displays six windows. *Six windows.* There's got to be a lot of bedrooms in this house. Brittany can't remember how many Jennifer said there were, but there should be enough so that she and Amanda don't have to share.

They pull up next to Nick's Jeep. Amanda puts the car in park and puts on the emergency brake (which they will definitely need on this steep hill) before shutting off the ignition, something Brittany feels like she and Amanda have done way too much of in one day. Hopefully, they can just relax and settle in tonight.

As they step out of the car to get their luggage out of the backseat and the trunk, Brittany begins to feel an overwhelming sensation of how peaceful and free it is up here. From the endless forests surrounding them to the birdsong to the patches of reddened sky illuminated by the setting sun high above the trees, it is astonishingly beautiful. They have a sneaking suspicion that they're going to like this place.

"Can you pop the trunk?" Brittany asks Amanda as she opens the back car door on her side to get her purse.

"Yeah, sure," says Amanda, looking down at the remote.

"Thanks," says Brittany, hearing it click open. She shuts the car door and walks over to the trunk to get her suitcase out of it. Amanda meets her there to get her own suitcase out once she's gotten her purse out of the backseat.

"Oh my God! You guys are finally here!" Brittany hears a voice up by the front door. They recognize it to be Kyle's.

"Kyle, hey!" Amanda says. Once she's gotten her suitcase out of the trunk, allowing Brittany to get her own, she heads the rest of the way up the driveway to see her friend.

"Do you guys need any help or anything?" Kyle asks them.

"I'm good, actually," Amanda tells him as she heads up the porch. "But thank you."

"Yeah, I'm good too," Brittany tells him, shutting the trunk now that she's gotten her suitcase out of it. She follows Amanda to the porch.

"Hey, you two," Brittany can now see Jennifer stepping out of the house to join Kyle on the front porch. "We didn't know when you guys were going to get here."

"Yeah, we weren't sure either," says Brittany, forcing a smile as she takes the small walkway before heading up the three steps to the porch. She stands and waits for Amanda to be done hugging Kyle so that she can hug him. She wonders if she should hug Jennifer too. They don't know each other that well. But before she has time to think it through, Kyle is ready for her. It's a quick hug, not the genuine hug that is characteristic of him. She wonders if something is bothering him. She selfishly hopes not, seeing as she has already endured more than enough in one day and really doesn't want to have to bother with anyone else's problems.

"Well, come on in," Jennifer tells them, holding the door open for them.

"Thanks for having us, Jennifer," says Amanda, following Brittany and Kyle inside the house.

Taking a look around, Brittany is amazed at how spacious and beautiful everything is inside the house. The stairs directly in front of them are made of the same shiny hardwood as the floors that they are standing on. The banister stretches past the top step and across the upstairs hallway. Behind the staircase is what looks to be the living room where they can see a giant sectional couch, in front of which is a large widescreen television. And in the office off to their left, they can see a large wooden bookcase lining the inside wall.

"Wow," says Amanda. "Your house is really nice."

"Thanks," says Jennifer, shutting the front door as she steps inside the house. "Here, so why don't you guys put your things upstairs? And then if you want, you can come down and have dinner with us—"

"Hey, guys. What's up?" Brittany hears Jeff's voice as she sees him and Nick coming into the foyer to greet them.

"Hey, Jeff," Amanda says to him.

"Did you guys have any trouble getting here?" Nick asks them.

"No," says Brittany. "It was actually pretty good. But it was good we had each other, though, in case something happened."

"Yeah, definitely," says Kyle.

"So I hope it's okay that we didn't wait up for you to start eating," says Jennifer. "We've just been really hungry. We haven't has anything to eat since, like, noon."

"Its fine," says Amanda. "It's just really nice that you cooked dinner in the first place."

"Yeah," says Jennifer. "Well, I know you guys are vegetarians. And I'm trying to become one and so is Nick." Jennifer looks over at Nick, who is rolling his eyes. "Um, do not roll your eyes at me, Nick. You remember I showed you those clips and you told me yourself that you wanted to stop eating meat."

Brittany, Amanda, Kyle, and Jeff laugh. Jennifer and Nick are always entertaining when they're together.

"You should have seen them in the car on the way here," Kyle tells Brittany and Amanda. "And you think Jeff and I bicker …"

"We didn't argue that much, Kyle," says Jennifer. "Anyway, so we bought a whole shitload of tofu and stir-fry at Wal-Mart on the way here."

"Yeah," says Jeff. "I didn't even realize Wal-Mart had tofu."

"It's the super Wal-Marts," says Jennifer. "Because they've got the grocery stores in them."

"This is so nice of you, Jennifer," says Amanda. "To be thinking of us like this."

"Yeah, well I'm not going to be cooking dinner for the rest of the week. We're going to be doing a lot of going out. But I just figured, since it's the first night, why not welcome you guys into my home."

"Well, it's still really sweet," says Amanda.

"Yeah, thanks," says Brittany.

"So the bedrooms are up there, obviously." Jennifer points up the stairwell.

"Oh, okay," says Amanda. "That's what I figured."

"Right, because that's where bedrooms typically are," says Jennifer, poking fun at herself. "So when you get up the stairs, you're going to see a door to your right. Just keep walking, because that's the master suite and my parents told me no one can sleep in there.

"But down the hallway, there are four bedrooms. Nick and I have the first bedroom on the left, and Kyle and Jeff have the first one on the right."

"Jeez, you have five bedrooms?" Brittany says.

"Yep," says Jennifer.

"Wow," Brittany says in amazement as she follows Amanda up the stairs.

"All right," says Kyle as he and the other three head back into the kitchen. "See you guys in a few minutes."

"Okay," says Amanda. "We'll be right down."

Once they have reached the top of the steps, Brittany and Amanda pass by the door that they now know to be the entrance to the off-limits master suite and start down the wide hallway, which stretches a surprisingly long distance.

"It feels like we're in a hotel," says Amanda, following Brittany down the hallway past their friends' bedrooms to get to their own rooms.

Once they've reached the final two bedroom doors, Brittany chooses the one to her right and opens it. As she steps inside, she is taken aback. Once again, she finds herself amazed by her surroundings.

There is a queen-sized sleigh bed on the right side of the room. Directly across from the bed is a cherry-wood dresser with a television on top of it. She can see that the wood of the dresser and the wood of the bed are the same color. There is a door on either side of the dresser. She figures one is the closet and the other is the bathroom. And at the end of the room is a large window that is only feet away in either direction from stretching from the floor to the ceiling. The window has lavish draping over it to block out the sun in the early morning when she will probably still be sleeping.

"Holy shit," she says. This beats any guest bedrooms she's ever seen before.

"And think," Amanda says to her after peeking inside of the bedroom. "This is just her parents' *vacation* house. Imagine what their actual home is like."

Brittany still stands in awe of the gorgeous bedroom in front of her.

"Well, I'm going to head across the hall," says Amanda.

Brittany nods her head in acknowledgment before heading over to the bed. Dropping her luggage to the floor in relief, she plops herself down onto the bed. *This is the life*, she thinks to herself. *The perfect escape.*

"So did you guys have a good day?" asks Kyle soon after Brittany and Amanda have come back downstairs and joined their four friends at the kitchen table for dinner. The kitchen is yet another room that Brittany is amazed by. It is filled with stainless steel appliances, maple cabinets, and waxed granite countertops. The table they are sitting at, however, seems a little out of place to Brittany. It is a simple wooden circular table, and as large as it is, it doesn't seem to fit in with the rest of the elegant, trendy furniture they've seen in this kitchen and throughout the rest of the house.

Brittany, who is starved from having had nothing to eat but a couple of Clif bars since breakfast, swallows a huge mouthful of the delicious tofu stir-fry before answering. "It was exhausting," she tells Kyle. *That's honest enough*, she thinks. She sure as hell is exhausted, both emotionally and physically.

"Are you talking about all the driving?" Nick asks her.

Brittany turns to Nick, who is seated next to her, and sighs before answering. "Yeah, that was a lot of it."

"How was your neighbor?" Kyle asks her.

"She was good," Brittany tells him. "It was nice to see her again." She wonders how much longer she is going to be able to keep the truth from Kyle and the other three.

"What about you guys?" asks Amanda. "How'd your day go?"

"It was all right," Kyle tells her, looking down at his plate of food.

"Did something bad happen to you guys?" Amanda asks. "I mean, you don't have to tell us if it's personal."

"No, it's fine," says Kyle. "I just got insulted by these guys when we were in Wal-Mart. They called me a 'faggot.'"

"Oh God," Amanda lets out a frustrated sigh. "Kyle, I'm so sorry that happened."

Brittany is frustrated by this too. She wonders how people get off treating others in such a way. Kyle is an amazing person.

He embraces who he is by being open about his homosexuality. He channels his individuality by spiking his hair and wearing eye makeup. And for all of this, he gets hated on? It's sickening the way some people are.

"I wish one of us was around when it happened," says Jeff. "I'll tell you right now if I was there they wouldn't have gotten away with it."

"The three of us were in the grocery part of the store when it happened," Jennifer explains to Amanda and Brittany.

"Yeah," says Kyle. "Like the naïve idiot I am, I decided it would be okay for me to go off alone in the store to get some hair gel. I guess I forgot what it's like outside of college, didn't I?"

Brittany doesn't really know what to say, and the others don't seem to either. The truth is harsh, and there's no beating around it. The world is a hateful place, and they're all here to live through it.

"I'm just glad you guys are so supportive of me," Kyle says, breaking the silence. Brittany can see that his eyes are filling with tears. "If I'd told my parents, they would have just told me it's because I need to man up or something."

"Yeah, well, screw your parents, Kyle," Jeff tells him.

"People are shit, man," Nick tells Kyle. "You just can't let it get to you, that's all."

"You make it sound so easy," Kyle says to Nick.

"Kyle, he's just trying to help," says Jennifer.

"Yeah, well, it's impossible not to let something like that get to you."

There is a brief, awkward silence before Jennifer suggests that they talk about something positive. Brittany figures that as the woman of the house, Jennifer probably sees it as her responsibility to keep things running smoothly and free of any unwanted negativity. "I mean, we've got this whole coming week to just enjoy ourselves," she says. "So we should really make the most of it."

"I completely agree with you," says Jeff.

"Yeah," says Kyle. "Sorry I'm such a downer."

"You have a right to be upset, Kyle," Jennifer reassures him. "I just want you be able to have fun here and not be depressed."

"Well, I'm really excited about being here," Amanda jumps in. "Everything about this place is just so surreal."

"I know," says Jennifer. "I love my parents for buying this place. Well, actually they bought the land and had the house built, but it's like, you can just come up here and get away from everything."

"Thank God for that," says Kyle.

"Yeah, but it's boring as hell," says Nick jokingly. "All the way up here in the middle of freaking nowhere."

"Yeah, like you would know," says Jennifer. "You've never even been up here before."

"Yeah, the only ones who have a right to say it's boring here are Jennifer and me," says Kyle.

"Right," says Jennifer, "and neither of us thinks that, do we?"

"Nope."

"I mean, there's seriously so much stuff that we can do," says Jennifer. "Like, just in the house, we've got the movie theater in the basement—Oh, and that's right. I should show you guys the basement."

"Yeah," says Kyle. "You guys have got to see the theater. It's fucking awesome."

"Yep," Jennifer agrees. "And then there's a lake nearby we can go swimming in. What else? ... Oh, there's this really neat town a few miles from here. They've got a whole bunch of restaurants, so we can maybe go to one each night. Or something like that."

"Well, Jennifer," says Jeff. "I'd just like to say I've never been more thrilled than I am now to be dating your ex-boyfriend." He puts his arm around Kyle.

Kyle rolls his eyes, causing Brittany and the other four to burst into laughter.

The vibe at the table is mutual. There is a strong sense among Brittany and her five friends that, despite some of their personal dilemmas, they are going to have a great time up here.

IT IS DARK NOW AS Russell drives down the road from the opposite direction in which he came when following them here. As he comes upon the break in the woods marked by the mailbox, his headlights enhancing his ability to see it, he slows his car. Shutting off the headlights, he turns up the gravel driveway.

He is thrilled at how easy this is going to be.

chapter 12

Once the dishes are cleared off the table and put into the dishwasher by Jennifer, it is time for Brittany and her friends to have some fun.

"So who wants to see the basement?" asks Jennifer, walking back over to the table where her five friends are seated.

"Oh, you want to go down?" says Kyle.

"Yeah, let's see the basement," agrees Jeff.

"Well, come on then." Jennifer waves them up from the table. "Let's go down and see it."

"Did you even show us pictures of the basement?" asks Amanda as she, Brittany, and the other three get up from the table and begin to follow Jennifer.

"You know what?" says Jennifer as she leads them past the table and to the small hallway that will lead them into what Brittany can see is the living room. "I think that's the one part of the house my parents left out when they sent me the pictures." Once she has started them down the hallway, she stops at a doorway to her left. "Okay, so here we are." She opens the door and steps out of the way. "You guys can all go down first," she tells them.

As Russell reaches the top of the driveway, which is much longer than he expected it to be—it's almost like another road—he can see two cars parked side by side in front of a large house. The one on the left he recognizes as Brittany's.

So all the drive leads up to is a single house. He figured this might have been the case. All the better that this is so.

Parking his car behind her Pontiac, he immediately shuts off the ignition. He doesn't want Brittany, her friend, and whoever else is up here hearing his engine and coming outside to see what is going on. He'd have to kill them right then and there, and he's not ready to kill anyone. Not yet.

Taking his key out of the ignition, he wonders how best to begin.

"I remember this," Kyle says once Brittany and the rest of the gang have reached the bottom of the stairwell. Kyle rushes over to what Brittany can see to be a mini-bar on their right.

Brittany and the three friends who haven't been down in this basement before are yet again wowed by what they see. Like the rest of the house, the basement is huge. To their right is the bar occupied by Kyle at the present moment. Straight ahead, past a set of sliding doors, they can see a large sofa and two comfortable-looking chairs forming a semicircle around a long, rectangular glass table that has magazines and an array of decorations on top of it. To the left of the sofa, chairs, and table, they can see a massive stereo system that includes an iPod portable speaker system cutely stationed at the very top. Further into the room, facing the glass doors to the outside, is a pool table. And to the left of the pool table, within a fair distance from one another, are two doors. The one closest to them is half open. The other is closed.

"So this is the basement," says Jennifer, stepping past her friends to take the lead.

"This place is the shit," says Nick.

"Is there any part of your house, Jennifer, that *isn't* incredible?" Amanda asks.

Jennifer laughs. "That's Kyle's favorite part," she says looking over at Kyle, who is now behind the bar's counter sorting through the cabinets for what there is to drink.

"You know me," says Kyle. "I love to drink."

"Yeah, and if it weren't for *me*," says Jennifer, "you probably *still* wouldn't have a clue about alcohol."

"Wow," says Kyle jokingly. "That was a really bitchy thing to say, Jennifer."

"You know me," she says smartly.

"So," she says, "let me show you guys the home theater."

"Oh, they're going to love this," says Kyle, stepping out from behind the bar to join Jennifer as she leads Brittany and the other three a little further into the basement to the pair of sliding doors.

"Here it is," says Jennifer, sliding open the doors and flicking on the light inside.

Stepping inside, Brittany and the other three take a look around. At the center of the theater are three rows of cushiony seats, four of the seats to a row. The walls are covered with posters of classic movies like *The Wizard of Oz, Psycho,* and *Edward Scissorhands.* And of course, how can they forget the movie screen? It takes up just about the entire inner wall. It is huge; it has to be nearly half as big as the screens at the actual movie theaters.

"Wow," says Jeff, wide-eyed.

"So we'll have plenty of time to watch movies in here," says Jennifer, sounding pleased by how thrilled everyone is. "Me or Kyle can show you guys how to work it later."

"You've got some rich-assed parents, girl," Nick says to her.

"Yeah, what kinds of jobs do they have?" asks Brittany, simply in awe of everything she has seen in the past hour.

"Oh," laughs Jennifer. "My dad's the CEO of an electric company and my mom's an interior decorator."

"Well, that explains the awesomeness of your house then," says Jeff.

"I'm jealous," jokes Amanda.

"I told you guys it would be wild up here," says Kyle.

"So," says Jennifer, heading out of the theater and into the main area of the basement. "Who wants to drink?"

"Count me in," says Kyle, following Jennifer out.

"We're going to have so much fun here," Amanda says to Brittany, Jeff, and Nick as they follow Jennifer and Kyle out of the theater and toward the bar. Amanda jumps up and down, looking to Brittany like a little girl who can't contain her excitement.

"Let's put on some music," says Jennifer, taking her iPod out of her pants pocket as she heads over to the stereo system. "Do you guys care what music we listen to?"

"Why are you going to use your iPod when you've got the whole fucking stereo system?" Nick asks her as he takes a seat at the rightmost stool at the bar.

"Because I can pick whatever I want," Jennifer says.

"It's called instant gratification, Nick," says Kyle behind the counter as he gets shot glasses out of the cabinet below and sets them down on the countertop alongside the bottle of Bacardi rum. "Hey, Jennifer, do you know if your parents have any Coke?"

"What, like cocaine?" Jennifer asks as she searches through the songs on her iPod.

"No, soda," says Kyle. Brittany and everyone else bursts out laughing as he opens the bottle of rum and pours it into the shot glasses. Kyle and Jennifer make an entertaining pair. "I figured, like rum and Coke instead of just hard liquor."

"Yeah, we have some from today," says Jennifer.

"Oh, I just didn't know if there was any down here," says Kyle. "Well, if you guys want *Coca Cola*, you know where to find it."

"Yeah, you got to think, Kyle," says Jeff, who is seated at the leftmost seat of the bar. Brittany is seated in between him and Nick, and Amanda stands alone on the side of the bar. "I mean, in the context of this situation, one could easily interpret 'Coke' to mean cocaine."

"Do you guys like 3OH!3?" Jennifer asks.

"Whatever you want, babe," says Nick. Seconds later, Brittany and her friends hear the beginning lyrics to 3OH!3's "Don't Trust Me."

"Let's part-ty!" Jennifer says over the music she's set to a suitably loud volume. Seeing that all of the bar seats are occupied, she dances her way over to Nick, who, at her insistency, moves the chair back for her so that she can get on his lap.

"Who wants to take the first shot?" Kyle asks now that all of the shot glasses have been filled.

"I'll take it," says Nick, picking up the shot glass nearest him and sending the liquor down his throat.

"Amanda, you shouldn't have to stand," Jennifer shouts over the music, which has now reached its chorus.

"It's fine," says Amanda.

"Do you want to take my seat?" Jeff offers her.

"No, it's okay."

"Yeah, we should have a chair right where you're standing," says Jennifer.

"Oh, Brittany's next," Kyle cheers Brittany on as she downs the shot.

Kyle is next to down a shot followed by Jennifer. Jeff is fifth, leaving Amanda as the only one who hasn't downed a shot, which Brittany and the others take instant notice of.

"Amanda, take the shot," Kyle urges her.

"I don't drink," she says to him.

"Still?"

"Why not?" Jeff asks her. "And don't tell me it's because you're underage."

Amanda laughs. "No, it's just I don't like how it tastes," she says. "And it makes me feel kind of depressed."

"Well, just take one shot then," Kyle presses on.

"Kyle, if she doesn't want to drink, don't make her drink," says Jennifer.

"All right, I'm sorry," says Kyle as he begins to fill up the empty shot glasses for a second round.

"No," says Amanda, reconsidering. "I—"

"Here, I'll make up for her," says Brittany, reaching past Jeff for the shot glass. She picks it up and downs her second shot.

"Damn," says Nick. "Someone wants to get drunk tonight."

"Jeez, Brittany," says Kyle as he refills the shot glass for her. "Make sure we can keep up with you." He takes a look over at Amanda. He can see that she looks a little hurt by what Brittany said. He hopes the two of them didn't have a fight on the way here and this isn't Brittany's way of lashing out at Amanda.

Brittany just laughs. Kyle figures she just wants to get drunk.

"Amanda, if you want to grab a Coke or something upstairs, feel free," says Jennifer before downing her second shot.

"Um, yeah, sure," says Amanda.

"I think I saw some bottles of water in one of these cabinets if you'd rather have water," Kyle suggests to her.

"Yeah, that's fine," she says. "I mean, I already had Coke for dinner, so I don't really need any more caffeine."

"And now she's worried about her caffeine intake," says Kyle as he pulls a room temperature bottle of water out of one of the bottom cabinets. "We need to find a way to loosen this girl up."

Jeff looks over at Amanda. "He's the same way to me," he tells her.

As Kyle stands back up and hands Amanda the bottle of water, he can see that Jennifer and Nick are getting cozy in each other's arms. They're whispering to one another about God knows what, probably something he and Jennifer never got to the point in their relationship to have whispered to one another.

"So do you guys want to go for a third round?" Kyle asks his four friends, seeing that the shot glasses are once again empty.

"We're actually getting kind of tired," says Jennifer. "I think the two of us are going to go up to bed."

"Oh, really," says Kyle skeptically. He looks up at the clock across the room. "It's 8:30."

"Yeah, well it's been a long day, man," says Nick.

"I'm getting kind of tired myself," says Jeff.

"Yeah, so we're going to go up now," says Jennifer, getting up off of Nick's lap and allowing him to stand as well.

"All right," Amanda says to them. "I guess we'll shut everything off when we go to bed."

"Yeah, that would be great," says Jennifer.

"And if you guys just want to hang out down here the next couple of hours," Nick says to them, "feel free."

"Okay," Jeff says suspiciously.

As Kyle sees them heading up the stairs hand in hand, he turns to his three remaining friends. "Real subtle." This causes his three friends to burst into smothered laughter.

"Are they seriously about to have sex?" Brittany asks him.

"Looked like it to me," says Kyle.

"Ew," says Amanda as she moves to the empty bar seat. "Like with us here?"

"So we're basically just stuck down here for the next two hours while they fuck their brains out?" Jeff asks.

Brittany bursts into laughter. "That's a great way of putting it, Jeff. A really great way of putting it."

"Yeah," says Jeff. "Like what if I actually want to go to bed?"

Kyle laughs. "I swear to you guys, if this was my place, I would not subject you to this kind of shit."

"I honestly never took Jennifer to be like that," says Amanda.

"Yeah, well then you don't know Jennifer," says Kyle.

"What?" says Amanda. "Was she always trying to have sex with you?"

Kyle looks over at Jeff. "Don't be jealous, Jeff." He turns back to Amanda. "I'll say she was definitely a horny girlfriend." His friends burst into laughter at this. "What? She was. But we never did anything."

"Yeah," says Jeff. "Because you're gay."

"Yet you and I haven't either … So what does that say about me? Oh, that's right. I don't consider sex a pastime."

"I can see we're going to be getting into some interesting topics tonight," Amanda says, laughing.

RUSSELL STANDS AT THE SIDE of the house where the wiring is located. He shines his flashlight on the wire he has just cut with the wire crimpers he now slides back into his coat pocket. He is proud of what he has accomplished so far, but he knows he still has a lot more to get done. But the best is yet to come.

They've all been hanging out down in that basement for the past half hour it seems. The fact that it's a daylight basement gave him the opportunity to sneak a peek through the back door. He had to be careful, though, to make sure no one saw him. He knew it wasn't too difficult, though, with him being dressed in all black. He matches the night.

There are six of them. This shouldn't be too hard, but he has to wait until they're not all together. He couldn't risk barging into the basement and shooting them up. What if a few of them got away? They could have called the police. It's best to wait until they're alone. And besides, where's the fun in rushing it? He's got all night.

Who did that little bitch think she was, coming and seeking him out like she did? He cannot wait for her to learn the consequences of what she has done. She never thought he'd come for her again. Well, she's going to be in for a big surprise. The monster in him has been revived, and after suppressing it for a half a decade, it feels better than ever. The urge is rampant.

Flicking off his flashlight and sliding it into the same coat pocket he put the wire crimpers in, he decides he ought to head back up to the front of the house. He's going to need to get into the house sometime. And now that everything is taken care of out here and they're all in the basement, he figures the best time for him to do it is now. The biggest challenges are going to be hiding out and keeping the first kills quiet so the others won't hear. He knows he isn't going to be able to use his pistol on every one of them, not the first at least. And definitely not Brittany.

He walks up the side of the house, and when he reaches the front, he makes a right, heading for the porch that stands only yards away from him. It's time to do this.

As he takes the steps up to the front porch, he is careful not to make any noise in case any of them have come up from the basement. He wouldn't want them hearing him, not after he's gotten this far. There is no turning back now, not that he ever considered that a possibility in the first place.

Once on the porch, before beginning to pick the lock, he peers into the sidelight to see if anybody is on the main floor. As soon as he does so, he jolts back, his heart beginning to pound.

There was a guy and a girl—the girl he'd only seen for the first time down in the basement—walking together down the foyer. It appeared as though they were about to head upstairs.

But none of this would have worried him if they both hadn't been looking right in his direction.

He collects himself, trying not to panic. Maybe they didn't see him. It was the worst timing imaginable, but they could have just been looking in his direction as the natural place for them to be looking at their angle.

He doesn't hear them inside. They're not starting any commotion. This brings him relief.

But he has to be sure. He needs to look into that sidelight again to see if they're still there, still looking in his direction, waiting for him.

Taking a deep breath and summoning the courage, he peers into the sidelight. Once he has done so, he takes a huge breath of relief.

They're gone.

"So what do you guys want to do now?" asks Kyle as he sits tiredly on the couch.

"Aren't we going to listen to some more music?" Jeff suggests across the room as he sorts through the music on Jennifer's iPod.

"Yeah, that's fine," says Kyle. "I just figured if you guys wanted to watch a movie on the big screen."

"Yeah, well, we've still got the rest of the night."

"Kyle, when do you think we should practice our lines while we're here?" asks Amanda, who is seated next to him on the couch.

"I don't know," says Kyle. "We've got all week. And no offense, Amanda, but I seriously do not want to be thinking about that stupid class right now."

"No, that's fine," Amanda reassures him. "We just obviously need to take some time with it."

"Yeah, we will. And thank God he's not making me be Willy the whole act. Because there's no way in hell I could memorize all those lines."

"Yeah, I know," Amanda agrees. "Who's doing Willy for the first half, though?"

"Dave."

"Oh, yeah. That's right."

"Yeah, I'm supposed to get in touch with him over break," says Brittany, who is seated in the end chair nearest the pool table. "He wants us to do our lines over the phone."

"You're Linda, right?" Amanda asks her.

"Yeah. Just for the first half of the act." Brittany takes a swig from the bottle of rum she's confiscated from the bar, feeling the burning aftertaste. She'll leave it to Dave to call her. She honestly couldn't care less about this play. She's got bigger things to worry about than memorizing a bunch of stupid lines for a grade. The alcohol has seeped into her system, but the things are still on her mind. What if there really is nothing left that can be done? Is Russell going to remain a free man? He did a horrible thing, and he needs to pay for it. He can't just get away with it because it was so long ago.

"Shit, there's no service on my phone," says Amanda.

"Yeah, that's how it is up here, unfortunately," Kyle tells her.

"Are you serious?"

"Yeah," says Kyle. "I mean, when we go into town later this week, there'll be service. But in the meantime, you're probably just going to have to depend on the landline."

"Well, I just wanted to know if my parents called me," says Amanda.

"I don't have any service either," says Brittany, taking another swig from the bottle once she has taken her phone out of her pants pocket only to see that there is no signal. She considered that this kind of thing might happen. She can e-mail Dave to let him know the deal. Screw him if he has a problem with it.

"Yeah, it sucks," says Kyle. "That's, like, the only downside about this place."

"I wish you or Jennifer would've said something about this before we came up here," Amanda says to Kyle.

"Sorry," says Kyle. "I completely forgot. But seriously, Amanda, even if you did know ahead of time, would you have passed this up?"

Amanda considers this for a moment. "Probably not."

"Well, there you have it then," says Kyle.

"I didn't know she liked Adam Lambert," they hear Jeff say.

"Oh, she's got Adam Lambert?" says Kyle excitedly.

"I love his music," says Amanda.

"Yeah, seriously," says Brittany. "Why the fuck didn't he win *American Idol*?"

"Because he's gay," says Kyle.

"That probably had something to do with it," says Brittany, slurring her words a bit. The buzz is now escalating to her becoming flat-out drunk, and she likes how it feels. It's finally starting to take everything away, everything she would otherwise be worrying about every waking minute. She doesn't need that kind of torture. She needs some peace of mind, no matter how temporary and consequential it is.

"Which music of his does she have?" Kyle asks Jeff.

"Oh, do you want me to go back?" asks Jeff.

"Here, let me come have a look," says Kyle, getting up off the couch and heading over to the stereo system. He takes the iPod from Jeff, who appears glad to hand it over to him.

"Oh my God! I love that song!"

"Which one is it?" asks Amanda.

"Fever."

"Fever?" Amanda tries to remember. "I don't think I've heard that one before."

"Well then, you guys need to hear it." Kyle puts the iPod back into the dock to play the song.

STANDING IN THE YARD, RUSSELL stares up at the room where a light has come on. He gave the guy and girl some time to get settled upstairs. Once he saw them head all the way up the staircase and down the hallway until he could no longer see them, he backed away from the sidelight and stepped off the porch to see if a light would go on in any of the rooms on the front side of the house. And to his luck, one has.

Now that they've gotten settled up there, should he go in? What about the other four? Could they possibly be coming up to bed soon?

How is he going to make this as neat and simple as possible?

As he suddenly hears music coming from what sounds like the basement, he now knows exactly what it is he is about to do.

This isn't how he planned it. It's even better.

chapter 13

Down in the basement, the music is blaring as Kyle backs away from the portable speaker system. He sees that Jeff is going to sit down in the end chair opposite where Brittany is seated. "Jeff!" he shouts in protest.

Jeff just turns and shakes his head no. Kyle knows he hates dancing.

"Fine!" says Kyle, beginning to dance on his own, feeling a little awkward and embarrassed to be doing so. He figures at least one of his friends, or boyfriend, would have some enthusiasm.

"I like this!" shouts Brittany as she forces herself up out of the chair with the bottle of rum in her hand.

Well, this is more like it, Kyle thinks to himself.

As Brittany begins to dance to the music alongside Kyle, he can see that she is struggling to stand upright. She has definitely achieved her goal of getting hammered. She smiles a drunken smile at him as she sways from side to side and takes a sip of the rum. After taking the bottle from her lips, her hand goes limp, causing the bottle to tilt sideways and allowing some of the rum to spill out of the bottle and onto the carpet.

"Shit," he says, taking the bottle from her and carefully setting it down on the coffee table. He picks the lid up off the table and screws it back onto the bottle to make sure no more of the liquor can spill out if one of them accidentally knocks the bottle off the table. Looking up from the table, he sees that Amanda and Jeff are laughing. *It's a good thing Jennifer isn't down here right now.*

"Dance with me!" Brittany shouts at Kyle, taking his arms and shaking them.

Kyle rolls his eyes, shoving aside the carpet incident for the time being. Standing back up, he sways from side to side with Brittany. Hardly anything spilled anyway, and the little that has spilled is hardly noticeable on the tan carpet. It's just a few wet spots.

As the song reaches its chorus, Brittany begins to jump up and down. She reminds Kyle of the rock stars on stage. It's funny how she has all this energy to be crazy like this when she's drunk. He guesses it's the numb factor.

Once the second verse has kicked in, Kyle invites Amanda to join in. She accepts, taking his hands as he helps her up off the couch. Jeff squeezes into his chair so that she can get by.

"Let's twirl!" Kyle shouts to her, taking her right hand with his. As the two of them spin around, Amanda accidentally knocks chins with Brittany, who she didn't realize was so close. "Oh my God! I'm so sorry!" Amanda shouts to her as she rubs her throbbing chin.

But Brittany doesn't seem to mind. The alcohol weighing her down, she falls to the floor in laughter.

"Are you okay?" Amanda asks her, but she can see that this was a dumb question as Brittany grabs hold of Amanda's arm, forcing her down to the ground with her. Obviously she's okay.

Physically, that is. Seriously, what is this, rough house? "Brittany, what the hell?" She laughs. It's obvious to Amanda that she is just trying to numb the pain that is coming from all that happened earlier that day. But still, waking up with a killer hangover, a guest in someone's house, isn't going to solve anything.

UPSTAIRS, JENNIFER CAN HEAR THE music blaring in the basement as she lies in bed with Nick, making out with him. She loves the taste of Nick's lips. And his tongue inside of her mouth makes a certain part of her tingle. The tingling is beginning to increase in its intensity too. She reacts to this sensation by rolling over onto Nick as he rolls onto his back so she can straddle him.

"Are we going to do this?" Nick asks her.

"Yeah," says Jennifer lustfully as she bends down to continue kissing him. She puts her hands in his and pushes both their hands against the headboard. As she feels Nick hardening under her, she sits back up and removes her shirt, revealing the satin red bra that she knows Nick loves to see on her. She tosses her shirt on the floor beside the bed. She loves it that Nick is as turned on as she is. It's what makes her even more turned on.

Nick picks his head up off the pillows and follows suit, removing his shirt and tossing it onto the floor. Jennifer hasn't seen a better chest than Nick's. It isn't too muscular, yet it's not too lean either. It's just right.

She can't wait for both of them to be naked, their bodies moving in rhythm to each other. And of course, the best part will be when they come. She loves how Nick's orgasms intensify her own, knowing that she's pleasuring him as well as herself.

As Nick falls back to the pillows, Jennifer runs her hands up and down his torso, feeling the firmness beneath his skin. His eyes are closed, and he is hardening even more. He is loving this. And she's about to make him love it even more.

Getting off of his lap, she bends back down and undoes his belt. Nick lifts his lower body up from the bed so she is able to pull the belt out of the pant loops. He then helps her get his pants unbuttoned and unzipped, after which she begins to pull them down to his ankles, revealing Nick's blue boxer briefs. She can see his penis bulging inside of his briefs. She reaches for the sides of the briefs to pull them down to his ankles as well—

She and Nick are startled out of their lust as they hear the doorknob being played with. Whichever one of their friends it is obviously can't get in since Nick shut the door and locked it as soon as they got into the bedroom.

"We're in here," shouts Nick, sounding extremely irritated at being interrupted.

Whoever it is doesn't give up. The two of them hear a loud bang at the door. It sounds like whoever is at the door is trying to force their way in.

Frightened and slightly annoyed by the bang, Jennifer moves to sit beside Nick, who has forced himself up from the pillows.

"What the fuck, man?" shouts Nick as he pulls his pants up over his briefs.

There is another bang, this time forcing the door open.

Jennifer and Nick sit in terror as they come to the realization that the person now stepping inside of the room with them is not any of their friends. It's an intruder. He is dressed all in black: black jacket, black leather gloves, black pants, and black shoes. They see, to their horror, that he is holding a pistol in his right hand.

"Nick." Jennifer grabs hold of Nick's arm as a useless form of protection.

"What do you want?" Nick asks the stranger.

Russell isn't interested in wasting any time with these two. He raises his pistol and shoots Nick square in the head.

"Oh my God!" screams Jennifer in horror as she sees blood splatter the wall behind them and Nick fall to the pillows, dead. This can't possibly be real. This has to be some kind of a nightmare. "Oh my—"

Russell fires his second shot at her head, killing her instantly. Her body falls to the pillows beside her boyfriend. He can see the smoke seeping out of the hole at the side of her forehead.

Two down, four to go. This is too damn easy.

"DID YOU GUYS HEAR SOMETHING?" Amanda asks after turning the volume down on the speakers.

"No," says Kyle, standing in between her and Brittany, who looks like she is about to fall over onto the chair she is standing beside.

"I thought I heard something," she says, listening to see if she can hear whatever it was again. It sounded like it was coming from upstairs. Maybe Jennifer and Nick are doing something. Oh, yeah, they're doing something all right. But it sounded to her like a boom, two of them. It couldn't have been gunshots.

"Turn it up," says Brittany, slurring her words.

Amanda obliges, assuming that whatever she heard is nothing to worry about.

chapter 14

Amanda feels herself drifting in and out of sleep. She is seated in the front row of the theater beside Jeff, Kyle, and Brittany. They are watching the movie *Thirteen*. They're at the middle of it. It's at the scene where Tracy and Evie are secretly leaving the movie theater to go and live it up with their friends. Amanda wishes she could keep watching, especially since some of her favorite scenes are still to come, but she's just too tired.

She glances over at Jeff and Kyle. It's so sweet, she thinks, when seeing that Jeff has his arm around Kyle, who has fallen asleep on Jeff's shoulder. She can see that Jeff's eyes are still open, but he looks a little tired too. It has been a long day for all of them.

"I'm going to go up to bed," Amanda tells Jeff.

"Yeah, we probably should too," says Jeff.

"You guys look so cute together," she tells him.

He smiles in response.

"All right. Well, I'll see you guys tomorrow," she says, forcing herself out of the comfortable chair. When she stands up, she can see Brittany next to Kyle. She lies in the chair curled up into the fetal position, deep in sleep. She looks so peaceful, given everything that just happened today. What a blessing sleep can be, a break from reality.

"Okay," says Jeff. "Sleep well."

"You too."Amanda turns and walks out of the theater, sliding the doors open and then shut behind her. In the main area of the basement, she looks up at the clock hanging on the wall to her right before going upstairs. She can see that it is just past ten. She isn't used to going to bed this early, but so much has happened today. She is exhausted. Yawning, she heads up the basement steps.

As she reaches the top of the steps and heads into the kitchen, she is taken by a strange feeling. She doesn't know what it means, but it makes her feel like something isn't right. She brushes the feeling aside, assuming it to be her own superstitions over being in an unfamiliar home in an unfamiliar area. She walks through the kitchen toward the stairs that lead to her bedroom, where she is sure she'll fall asleep in no time.

At the bottom of the steps, she can see that the upstairs hallway light is on. *Good*, she thinks. She doesn't have to worry about feeling her way to her bedroom in the dark.

She starts up the stairs. Climbing the steps is an effort. *I just want to get to my room already,* she thinks to herself. She knows that she has to brush her teeth, wash her face, and get into her pajamas still, none of which she feels like doing. Maybe she can skip washing her face, because she really has to get to sleep before she starts feeling less tired. Because once she feels less tired, it'll take forever for her to fall asleep, despite how tired she really is.

When she finally reaches the top of the steps and starts down the hallway, she notices that the light is on and the door is slightly ajar in the first bedroom on the left. Jennifer and Nick must still be awake. She'll wish them good night. Hopefully, she won't catch them in the middle of something, though. She doesn't want to embarrass them or herself.

As she reaches their door, she knocks lightly, causing the door to open a little so that she is able to peer inside. Upon doing so, she takes a step back.

She can see blood splattered all over the wall behind the bed. She sees Nick and Jennifer, both lying completely still on the bed. She knows that they are dead because she can see the bullet hole in Nick's forehead, his eyes open wide. Jennifer's head is beside Nick's chest. Her blood has soaked what had been her beautiful blonde hair.

"Oh my God!" sobs Amanda. *This can't be real*, she thinks to herself. "Oh my fucking God!" A feeling of vulnerability rushes through her. She is next. She knows it. Whoever did this is up here waiting for her, waiting to put a bullet into her head just like he did to Jennifer and Nick. She has to get downstairs, to be with her three friends so she can warn them. There is nothing she wants less than to be alone up here.

Suddenly, she feels a gloved hand wrap around her mouth. She feels herself being roughly pulled backward so that she is pressed up against the chest of whoever this person is. Out of the corner of her eye, she can see that her captor is pulling the gun out of his coat pocket. As he presses it up against the side of her head, she lets out a smothered scream. It was idealistic of her to think she had a chance. She knows that her screams will do no good; it is pure instinct. She expects to be dead at any moment, brutally murdered just like the other two.

But instead of shooting her in the head, he begins to drag her into the bedroom by the jaw. As soon as they are both all the way in the bedroom, he kicks the door shut behind them. She continues to scream through his hand. Now she isn't just screaming out of fear but because the pain of having her jaw gripped like this is excruciating. She is blinded by the tears that are beginning to fill her eyes.

As they reach the bed, she is extremely relieved to feel his grip loosen on her jaw. What is he going to do to her? Is he going to shoot her here? But he's putting the gun down. He's putting the gun down on the bed. She can try to reach for it, but it's closer to him than to her, and what if he gets to it first and decides to shoot her with it?

While Amanda knows that she cannot get to the gun without things turning more violent than they already are, she is no longer overcome by fear, deemed powerless. On the contrary, she is experiencing a rush of adrenaline, a rush that is telling her to fight back.

With all of her might, she pulls the man's hand away from her mouth, twisting his arm and freeing herself in the process. She then elbows him in the stomach. She can hear him groan in pain, but there is no time to wait for a reaction. She has to get out of this room. She immediately darts for the entrance to the bedroom.

"You fucking bitch!" she hears him yell.

Amanda fumbles with the doorknob for a second before getting it opened.

And then she hears the gunfire. This slows her down. How can she get away from this man if he is shooting at her?

But miraculously, she hasn't been hit. She is in disbelief. But she can't be distracted. She runs out of the bedroom and down the hallway to the stairs. She has to get to her friends so she can lead them out the back door she remembers seeing in the basement. They can hide out in the woods. There's no time to call 9-1-1.

She is expecting to be shot at any moment as she charges down the steps, trying her best not to slip and fall due to her speed. "Oh my God," she can hear herself saying over and over again under her breath.

Then she hears a second gunshot. "Help me!" she screams and feels the vibration of the bullet hitting the wall only a few feet above her. She needs to get down the steps. *Please God,* she prays. *Please don't let him kill me.*

When she has finally reached the bottom of the steps without being shot, she makes a sharp u-turn for the basement, hoping that she has surprised the man by not running to the front door. Hopefully, this will give her some time to get her and her friends out of here—that is, if he doesn't already know she is heading for the basement. She hopes and prays that he doesn't.

Running through the kitchen, Amanda makes the turn down the small hallway for the basement entrance. Seeing that the door is still open, she races down the steps. She has no idea how close he is behind her. She doesn't have time to turn around and see. She needs to get away.

At the bottom of the steps, Jeff startles her. He just looked like he was about to hit her over the head with the glass vase he is clutching for protection. "Amanda, what the fuck is happening?" he asks her.

"We have to go," she says, looking over to Brittany and Kyle, who are standing together just outside of the entrance to the theater. They look terrified. "Come on," she says, running through the basement toward the glass doors leading to the outside.

As her three friends turn to follow her, they hear a gunshot behind them. They see the bullet hit the wall beside the glass door Amanda has now reached and is trying to get opened. They see her turn the latch and slide the door open all in a second's time. She flees from the house before the gunman has another chance to shoot at her.

Kyle is first to turn to see who it is that fired the shot. He sees that the gunman now has his gun aimed at the back of Jeff. "Jeff!" he screams, desperately hoping to warn him before it's too late.

The man wastes no time at firing a shot at Jeff. It sends him to his knees, the vase dropping to the floor beside him.

"No!" screams Kyle.

"Kyle, come on." He feels Brittany tugging at his arm in the direction of the door, but he isn't going anywhere. Not without Jeff.

He sees the man move his gun down so that he can put the barrel of his pistol to the back of Jeff's head. "Oh, please God, no," Kyle sobs.

"Kyle, we have to go." He can feel Brittany tugging at his arm even harder this time. "Come on."

He knows that there is nothing he can do to save Jeff. The man has a gun at his head, and in any moment he will fire. Kyle doesn't want to see what this sick human being is about to do to the person he has come to love more than anything. He begins to follow Brittany to the doors.

It's only seconds later that Kyle feels a sharp, searing pain in his back. It hurts like nothing he has ever felt before. It doesn't take him more than a moment to realize in horror that he has been shot.

"Oh my God, Kyle," Brittany says in shock as she turns

and sees that Kyle has been hit. She sees his face turn pale and his legs begin to wobble. As he begins to fall, she catches him in her arms and kneels down to the floor with him, not knowing what else to do.

Russell steps past Jeff to get a closer aim. As he does so, he shoots her friend in the back a second time. He is content at seeing the amount of blood spurting out.

"Stop it!" Brittany sobs.

Russell turns back to Jeff. He is still on his knees, helpless but not dead. Russell shoots him a second time, this time in the chest.

AMANDA RUNS FOR HER LIFE through the woods surrounding the house. It is difficult to see where she is going. The only light she has to see by is coming from the house that she is now distancing herself from at a rapid pace.

She heard the second, third, fourth, and fifth shots. It's bad. She knows that. But she doesn't have time to think about it. She has to focus on saving herself.

The only noises she hears now are her own heavy breathing and footsteps, accompanied by the snapping of twigs and the rustling of leaves.

Where is she going? She has no idea. She is in the middle of nowhere, soon to be lost in the woods, she assumes.

All she knows is that she doesn't want to die.

chapter 15

"Why are you doing this?!" Brittany screams at the man.

"You don't remember me, do you, Brittany?" he asks her.

Brittany still holds Kyle in her arms. She can see that he is beginning to gurgle as the blood rushes to his mouth. She knows that these are probably his last moments. He is losing an immense amount of blood, and she can feel the wetness seeping through his clothes and onto her shirt. He needs to get to a hospital fast, but she knows, with the gunman standing over her, that there is no way that this will even be a possibility.

She stares up at the gunman as the tears run down her face. She expects to be shot by him at any moment and wonders what he is waiting for, why he hasn't done it already.

Then it hits her. How does he know her name? And why would she remember him?

It's *him.* "No," she says in denial. This can't be happening. There is simply no way that this is possible. "No." How could he have possibly known? And then found her?

"*No!*" she shouts as he comes at her with his gun pointed

at her head. As she backs up so she can get up to make a run for it, she is forced to let go of Kyle, insensitively allowing him to fall to the floor.

But Russell is too quick for her. "*No!*" she shouts again as she feels the pain of Russell grabbing her by her hair as he forces her up from the ground.

Once he has her all the way up, she feels a very temporary relief as Russell lets go of the chunk of her hair before pressing her up against his chest. "Now," he says into her ear, pressing the gun up against the side of her head, "you're going to help me find your fucking friend. Walk."

Brittany can feel him loosening his hold on her and his motioning her forward. Through her sobs, she looks behind her to see if he still has the gun pointed at her head.

"Walk," he says.

The tears rushing to her eyes again, she turns back and begins walking toward the slightly ajar back door. She is both terrified and shocked out of her mind.

AMANDA CONTINUES TO RUN THROUGH the woods, trying her best not to trip and fall. She is getting exhausted. She doesn't know how much longer she can run. To her relief, she knows that she isn't being chased after by the gunman. He is back in the house with her friends … She doesn't want to think about it. She has to find a way out of these woods to a road where she can get help.

She slows to a stop, bending over to rest her hands on her knees. She is completely out of breath, and her heart is pounding like it never has before. She pulls her phone out of her pocket to see if, by some miracle, there is a signal. "Shit," she says after seeing that there is still no service. She's got to find some way to get help. Jennifer said there's a town a few miles from here. And she and Brittany passed some houses about five minutes before they got here. Could she try to run to them?

No more running. She can't take it anymore. What about one of their cars? But she'd have to go back into the house and get the keys. And that's where the gunman is. If he spots her, he'll kill her. She's lucky enough to have gotten away just now. She isn't going to take another chance on her life.

She is suddenly overcome with a feeling of dizziness, which she is sure has to do with all the running. Feeling safe enough for the moment, she sits down in the dirt and leans up against the nearest tree. She wraps her hands around her legs and begins to sob like a helpless child. *This is awful*, she thinks to herself. All of her friends are probably dead. It is only a matter of time before the killer comes looking for her. She feels like she should just give up, that she should just head back out of the woods to her death because she is bound to die tonight anyway. She might as well get it over with.

But then the adrenaline kicks back in. *I'm not going to die tonight*, she tells herself. She will do everything in her power to stay alive.

BRITTANY LEADS RUSSELL OUT FROM the back of the house and toward the surrounding woods. There is a little hill of grass to go down first before the woods begin. She fears how dark it will be once they get so far into the woods that the light coming from the house will be only a distant flicker.

"Call her," Russell demands, touching the barrel of the gun to the back of her head.

"Amanda," Brittany calls out, hating what she is being forced to do.

She feels the sudden force of him grabbing her from behind as he presses the gun up against the side of her head. "Louder."

This time, out of sheer fright, Brittany screams her friend's name. She is tempted to scream "Help me!" but stops herself just before she utters the words. Russell would kill her. She desperately hopes that Amanda, wherever she is, hears her and can pick up on what is going on so that she can find a way to help.

WAS THAT BRITTANY? AMANDA JUST heard a scream. *Oh, thank God. Brittany is still alive.* She has to find her and bring her to safety before *he* catches up to her.

She hurriedly forces herself up off the ground and reluctantly begins to tiptoe back toward the house to see if she can spot Brittany and get her attention.

She hears Brittany screaming for her again.

She can't take the silence. She has to call back, to give Brittany some idea of where she is. She can't just let Brittany keep calling for her. What if Russell hears her and comes after her?

She is getting closer to the house. Through the brush, she can now get a better glimpse of the house lit up by the spotlight.

Hearing another of Brittany's screams, she can tell that Brittany is now closer to her than she was before—much closer. Is it safe to respond now? She thinks it is. But where exactly is Brittany?

It is at this precise moment that she feels as though her heart is about to stop. She sees Brittany and then the gunman, who has his pistol pressed up against the back of her head. They can't be anymore than twenty feet away from her.

Amanda realizes exactly what is going on. She has to get further back into the woods, back to where she was.

But is it too late? Have they seen her? She looked *right at them.*

Holding her breath in fear of what is to come, she slowly and quietly as possible backs up a few feet and turns to kneel down behind the nearest tree. Is this the moment when she is going to die?

Hearing Brittany screaming for her again, she feels tremendously relieved to know that she hasn't been spotted. She's still got a fighting chance.

"How DID YOU KNOW TO find me here?" Brittany asks Russell as they continue their trek into the woods.

"I have my ways," says Russell.

"So how'd you figure out I was onto you?" she asks him. She knows he saw Anne at the bank, saw that she recognized him. But how did he know that Brittany was back in town? How did he find her? Was he watching Anne's house to see if she would show up?

"Let's just say if you're going to try to track someone down, you'd better be a whole lot more fucking discreet about it. Keep calling her."

He had to have seen them at Anne's, Brittany figures. So had he followed her and Amanda up here? How the hell had he managed to do that without either her or Amanda realizing someone was following them? How could they have been so oblivious?

"I want to know something first," she says, turning to face him. What's he going to do, shoot her? He needs her to lure in Amanda.

"Yeah, and what is that?" Russell asks.

"Why me?" she asks him. "Why my mom? What did either of us ever do to you?"

Russell laughs. "What do you want, an apology? All right then. I'm sorry. I'm oh so very fucking sorry."

"I don't want an apology. I just want to know why."

"You've got a lot of nerve, girl. Trying to track me down like you did, and now here you are trying to have a heart to heart. Well, you know what? I don't fucking *appreciate* having my life turned upside down by you and that fucking neighbor of yours." He waves the gun at her, causing her to flinch. "You better be thanking me for not blowing your fucking head off this very second."

Although she can't help but flinch over Russell waving the gun at her, Brittany isn't as intimidated by the gun as she was. She's pretty sure he isn't about to shoot her. He needs her.

"*Your* life turned upside down?" she says. "How about the way you turned *my* life upside down? You killed my mom." She can feel her anger and disgust toward this man rising to the surface. She knows she isn't going to be able to contain herself. "So don't you *ever* tell me about turning your life upside down, you filthy fucking piece of shit!" On impulse, she grabs hold of his shoulders and knees him with all her might in the groin. She doesn't wait to see if it affects him. She reaches for the gun in his right hand and tries to grab hold of it. She wants to kill this man. She wants to blow *his* head off.

153

But before she has a chance to even come close to getting the gun, Russell frees his hand from her grasp and whips her in the face with his pistol. Before she has a chance to process what has just happened, before she has a chance to process the immense pain in her cheekbone, he whips her with the pistol again, this time even harder. As she struggles to stand upright from pain of the blows, he jumps down onto her, forcing her to the ground.

"Get off of me!" she screams at him, fighting the pain in her cheekbone. She can't believe this is what has happened. She wanted so badly to get that gun from him.

"Is *this* what you wanted?" Russell aims the pistol at her face. "Huh? Is *this* what you fucking wanted? Well, it's mine."

"Please," Brittany sobs, disgusted by his spit that has hit her face. There is no denying now that she is completely at his mercy.

"Do you hear me, bitch?!"

"Yes. Please." She can feel the tears running down the sides of her face.

"All right then," Russell says. "Now get up."

As she struggles to get up off the ground, her back in pain from the hard fall, she feels an upset starting in her stomach. The upset wastes no time in moving up to her chest. She knows what this is. She's about to vomit. She turns to her side as she feels the bile rush up her throat and into her mouth. She wretches into the dirt, her eyes blinded by the tears brought on by the gagging.

Along with her sudden onset of sickness, which she imagines the liquor she drank is a big contributor of, she is in shock. She can't believe that he didn't kill her after what she just did. She thought she could have overtaken him, but she failed miserably. So why hadn't he killed her? Sure, he may have wanted her around at first for the fun of finding Amanda, but after what she just did ... she can't believe she is still alive.

AMANDA IS RELIEVED AS SHE hears Brittany and the gunman begin to head further away from her into the woods. But she is also terrified for Brittany. What is going to happen to her?

She is in disbelief at the conversation she just heard between Brittany and the gunman. It can't be Russell Thompson. That is impossible. There's just no way.

She shakes off the implausibility for the time being and gets into focus what needs to be done at this very moment. She needs to get back to the house to call for help. What awaits her when she gets there, she doesn't want to know.

chapter 16

Amanda can see that the back door to the basement is fully open now as she rushes to it. As she steps inside, she shuts the door behind her and locks it. What if they come back? She isn't about to just let them walk right in.

After locking the door, she rushes past the pool table and heads to the phone she remembers seeing on the end table next to the couches.

But before she gets to the phone, she feels a knot tie in her stomach as she sees Jeff across the room, leaned up against the wall in between the bar and the stairwell. His head is turned to the side, and she can see that his eyes are open. Seeing a trail of blood before him, she knows he must have crawled over there in the hopes of remaining conscious. But he died instead.

At the same time, she sees Kyle lying on his stomach on the floor beside her. He is still.

She rushes over to Kyle and kneels down beside him. She can see that his eyes are open as well, causing the knot in her stomach to increase in its tightness.

"Kyle," she says, shaking his body from side to side in desperation. "Kyle."

She can see the blood that had been running out of his mouth and onto the carpet is now beginning to dry up. His shirt that had earlier in the evening been gray is now a blackish red.

She isn't ready to accept that he is dead. He can't be dead. First Jennifer and Nick and now Jeff and him? No. She can't accept it. "Kyle." She shakes his body back and forth. "Wake up, Kyle." She shakes him again, harder, and feels her hands becoming wet from the blood saturating his shirt.

Nothing. Still the motionless body he was when she found him here just a minute ago.

"Please don't let him be dead. Please, God, don't let him be dead." She's never been the religious type, but she is desperate now. If there is a God, then she needs him. She needs him to bring her friend back to consciousness.

Still, he will not wake up. He is dead.

"Wake up!" she screams out, shaking him uncontrollably. "Wake up, wake up, wake up!" She can feel her heavy sobs pulsating through her. She doesn't care if he—Russell, or whoever he is—can hear her in here. She has to give up now. She doesn't know how she can possibly go on with all of her friends dead like this. She could handle Jennifer and Nick, although it was horrifying to see them like that. But not Kyle, not one of the closest friends she's ever had, a person who she couldn't help but give a part of her soul to.

Let Russell, the gunman, whoever he is, come in. Let him find her like this and shoot her dead. She doesn't care anymore. It is too much to bear. Too much.

Through her sobs, she hears a noise that forces her away from her inner agony. She turns to see where the noise is coming from, and off to her left, past the couches and the stereo system, she sees that it is Jeff. He's calling for her. He's calling for her to help him. He is alive. She takes a deep breath. This is rough, and brutally so. Nothing in her life has ever prepared her for something like this. She could never have possibly imagined the absolute horror of this situation. It is unreal. But despite all of this, she feels a sense of strength within her. It's the adrenaline yet again. It's telling her that she can make it out of here, that she can survive.

"Amanda." She can hear Jeff calling out for her again. He is now moaning in agony.

She forces herself up from the floor, realizing that she needs to call 9-1-1, and fast. He can't die also. Maybe she really *can* get through this, just as long as no more of her friends die.

"Jeff, I'm going to call 9-1-1," she tells him, rushing over to the phone. She can hear him continuing to moan.

She picks up the phone and presses the talk button. She doesn't bother listening for the flashing before dialing 9-1-1. She puts the phone to her ear, impatiently waiting to hear the ringing. She waits a second and then another. "Come on," she whispers to herself in frustration.

Ten seconds later and still nothing. "Ah, fuck." Maybe she did something wrong. She presses the flash button down at the bottom and puts the phone to her ear again … no flashing noise. Maybe that's what was wrong.

She puts the phone back on the charger to hang it up. "Please, come on." It had better work this time. She can feel the buildup of stress in her chest.

She waits a couple of seconds before picking the phone up again. This time, after pressing the talk button, she listens for the flashing noise … nothing.

"He cut the phone line, didn't he?" suggests Jeff.

Amanda checks to see if the phone is plugged in. She looks behind the couch and sees to her dismay that the plug is in the outlet. "Fuck," she whispers to herself, hanging up the useless phone. Jeff is right. That sick bastard cut the phone line. Now what are they going to do? She is beginning to feel another buildup of panic, but she suppresses it, knowing she can't lose it. She needs to keep it together. For Jeff. For Brittany. She realizes that it is now up to her to get them out of this alive.

The car. She can use Brittany's car to get her and Jeff to the nearest home, gas station, or whatever they come upon first to call for help. And maybe she can even get service on her phone on the drive.

"He cut the phone line," she can hear Jeff saying again. Not only is his voice slurred, but it is beginning to sound panicky. "We're going to die, aren't we?"

Amanda heads over to him. As she does so, she takes her hair tie off of her wrist and ties her hair up into a bun. She'll need her hair out of the way for this.

"We're going to die," he says again. He is tearful. "Kyle's dead, and now we're going to die too."

As Amanda reaches him, she kneels down beside him and looks into his wandering eyes, which are filled with terror and panic. "Jeff, look at me," she tells him.

"What are we going to do, Amanda?"

"I'll tell you what we're going to do. We're going to go up those stairs,"—she points up at them—"we're going to get in Brittany's car, and we're going to drive somewhere to get help. Okay? But you have to promise me you're going to stay strong."

"What about Brittany?"

159

What about Brittany? Amanda wonders. Russell has her, and he's armed. They're better off driving off and getting help for her as opposed to risking their lives to try to rescue her on their own. Well, rather Amanda risking *her* life. What good would Jeff be?

"Here," she says to him, putting her arms on either side of his torso. This is going to be excruciating for both of them.

Jeff groans in pain as they both work to get him up.

"Come on, Jeff. We can do this." She can't help but be a little repulsed by the wetness of the blood-soaked shirt that she is pressing her hands into. But she is determined to get them both out of here and to safety.

His weight is beginning to be too much for her. "Jeff, come on," she tells him. "I can't do this all by myself."

"I can't," says Jeff, falling back to the floor in pain. "It's too much."

Amanda is beginning to get angry. "Yes, you can. You can do this."

"I can't."

She can feel a lump forming in her throat from the frustration of this. She wants to cry again. Not only that, but she is terrified that at any moment Russell and Brittany will come walking through that back door after forcing it open. And then Russell will see her and Jeff, and he'll kill them.

"Jeff," she says, "I'm not going to leave you here; do you understand me? I'm not going to let you die here. But you *have* to help me. Now, get … the fuck … up." She places her hands on his torso and summons all the strength left in her to get him up off of this floor. She is glad to hear Jeff moaning. It means he's trying now.

"Come on, Jeff," Amanda encourages him. "Come on."

His ass is off the ground now. She realizes that she should push up on it to make sure he doesn't fall back down again. In any other situation, this would be awkward. But not now. That kind of stuff has no importance now. So that's exactly what she does. *Just don't let him fall back down,* she tells herself. *Don't let him fall back down.*

And finally, he's up and standing. Before he has a chance to fall back down, she wraps his arm around her so she can support his weight. "Hold on to me, okay?" Now she can feel his weight. And for a second, she feels like *she* can't do this. But the shock of his weight settles in a little so that it becomes bearable, but only just so.

And now, they have to get up the steps. If it weren't for Russell being somewhere outside of this house, she'd without a doubt choose the basement door as their means out. They'd walk around the house to the car. But that can't happen. They've got to get up these steps.

"Come on," she tells him as she places her foot on the first step. "We can do this."

"WHERE ARE YOU, YOU LITTLE cunt?!" Russell shouts out into the night.

Brittany's voice is hoarse from all the calling out to Amanda Russell has been forcing her to do. While she hopes he won't make her call out anymore, she is terrified of what will happen once he gives up looking for Amanda, once she is no longer of use to him. Will he kill her and leave her body in these woods? She knows he will kill her eventually. So should she try to overtake him again? Hell, no. He's too strong for her. Should she try to make a run for it then? It's better than not doing anything. Maybe she can get away. But she won't know if she doesn't try. She won't live to know.

"It's time to go back," says Russell.

"What?" Brittany assumes he means back to the house, but what for?

"You heard me. Let's go."

Brittany sees him motioning his gun in the direction of the house. "But what about Amanda? Don't you want to look for her still?"

"Don't play games with me, bitch," he says. "We both know damn well you're happy as fuck I haven't found her. Now let's go." He motions his gun toward the house a second time.

Brittany doesn't move. She needs to find a way to escape from this man. Are there any broken off branches on the ground? She can hit him over the head with one of them. It's not as hard to see as she thought it would be, considering that they are now hundreds of feet away from the house, which emanates their main source of light to see by. The leaves from the trees fail to conceal the almost-full moon in the sky that shines down on them.

If she expects to make an escape, she has to distract him with something. Until she figures out how to do this, she needs to stall him with conversation.

"What happens when we get back to the house?" she asks him.

"That's for you to find out."

Without moving her head, she looks below her for any branches. She spots a good-looking one to her left. It is pretty thick in diameter and not too long. It probably won't do enough to knock him out, but it'll surely knock the wind out of him.

"Are you going to kill me?" she asks him. She's just thought of something. She knows how she's going to distract him.

"Oh, I'll kill you, all right."

"Wouldn't it be easier if you just killed me here?" She eyes the branch.

"Do you want to me to kill you here? Well, all right then." He aims the gun at her.

"Amanda, run!" Brittany screams, looking past Russell.

"What the fuck?" Russell looks behind him in a confused state. As he does so, Brittany doesn't waste any time in picking up the branch, and as he turns back around, having realized oh too quickly, she fears, that she was just fooling him, she whacks him on the shoulder.

She then drops the branch and runs. Why didn't she hit him in the head? She is frustrated with herself for having panicked. She was afraid he'd caught on. Well, now he's definitely caught on.

Where is she running? She doesn't know exactly. Just away from Russell. Somewhere far enough away so that Russell can't find her. Ideally, back to the house where she can call for help. But she is running in the wrong direction for this. She is running just to get away.

She can hear him chasing after her at lightning speed. She can't let him catch her, though, because if he does, she knows she'll be in for it. She can't help but slow down at times, though, to make sure that she doesn't slam into the tree trunks all around her. Despite the moonlight, it is hard to see where she is going.

Suddenly she feels a throbbing pain in her head. It takes her a second to realize that she's just hit her face against a tree trunk, exactly what she was trying to avoid. Her eyes begin to water, and she starts to lose focus because of the pain. She can't stop now, though. She needs to keep running—

She feels her hair being grabbed from behind her, and in a swift motion her head is pushed forward. And then ... Nothing.

Russell allows her to fall to the ground, unconscious. Although some of his anger toward her is now relieved, he can't help but be tempted to shoot her dead right here, right now. But he knows it will be more satisfying to save her for last. Let her see the damage she's brought on herself and her friends. Let those be her very last thoughts.

It's time to take her back to the house, now. Despite having to drag her dead weight, at least he won't have to worry about her fighting back.

AMANDA HAS FINALLY, MIRACULOUSLY, GOTTEN herself and Jeff to the top of the steps. Getting up those steps was a tremendous effort for the both of them. She feels immense relief, realizing that the hardest part is behind them. Now all they have to do is get the keys to one of the cars and drive to the nearest location where they can call the police. The police will take it from there.

She fears for Brittany, though. It is only a matter of time before she is killed. She desperately hopes that she'll still be alive by the time the police arrive. The chances, unfortunately, are slim. But she has save Jeff and herself.

"Nick's keys are on the table by the front door," says Jeff.

"Okay," says Amanda, not caring whose car they drive. "Just keep holding onto me, Jeff. We're almost there." She says this not only for Jeff's sake but for her own. She is physically exhausted. By saying aloud that they're almost to the car, she is helping herself make it to the car without falling to the floor and forfeiting in the process.

They trudge down the small hallway and through the kitchen toward the front door, every new step being a greater effort than the one before. They're almost there, though. They're almost there.

When they get to the front door, they see to their relief that the keys are on the side table just as Jeff said. *He* hasn't done anything with them, thank God. Amanda pockets the keys so she can use her free hand to open the front door.

But before she opens the door, she peers out the sidelight to see if he might be out there with Brittany, waiting for the two of them. As far as she can see, there is no one in sight, but she is still cautious when opening the door.

As they step out onto the front porch, she shuts the front door behind them. She doesn't want Russell to think anything is different than he has mistakenly assumed it to be. But does it really matter at this point? Not if they're about to drive off. Russell will see that the car is gone, and he'll know. But hopefully he won't come to the front of the house to notice that the car is gone. Because if he does, then he will no longer have any use for Brittany. And then he'll probably kill her.

As they step down onto the first porch step, Jeff notices first. Amanda picks up on it shortly after. She can see that body of the Jeep is lower to the ground than it is supposed to be. She can also see the flattened, worthless front tires.

"What are we supposed to do now?" panics Jeff.

Amanda turns to Brittany's car, which is parked next to the Jeep. Can she leave Jeff on the porch really quick so that she can go back into the house and get Brittany's keys out of her room where she hopefully has them?

But she doesn't think this through any further as she sees that Brittany's tires have also been slashed. "Oh, fuck," she whispers under her breath. This man is determined to kill them. First the phone and now this. She should have known. How are they going to get out of this? *Are* they going to get out of this?

"We need to use his car," says Jeff.

Behind Brittany's car, Amanda can see another vehicle. Obviously, it's Russell's. "How the hell are we going to do that, Jeff, if we don't even have his keys?" What the hell are they going to do? Is there anything they can do at this point?

She and Jeff are frightened out of their present conflict as they suddenly hear footsteps in the woods off to their right. "Fuck," says Amanda. He's coming this way, and he's going to see them. And he's going to kill them. Can they go back into the house and hide? This would be easy enough if it was just Amanda, but she's got Jeff to worry about.

She realizes, though, that going back into the house serves no purpose anyway. That is where Russell and Brittany are most likely headed. They must have given up looking for her in the woods and have come back to the house to find her.

"Come on," she tells Jeff.

"What, why?"

"Just trust me, okay?" She helps him down the rest of the steps. As the footsteps become more audible, she hurries herself and Jeff toward the Jeep. Their feet on the asphalt are far too noisy.

As they get behind the side of the Jeep furthest from where the sound is coming, Amanda notices Jeff peering over the side of the car. "Jeff, what are you doing?"

"I don't think they're coming this way," he says.

"What?"

"It sounds like they're headed toward the basement."

"Oh, shit."

"What? What's wrong?"

"He's going to see you're not there."

"Oh, fuck, and he's going to come out here looking for us, isn't he? What the fuck are we going to do now? We're going to die. We're going to fucking die."

Trying to ignore Jeff's onslaught of panic for her own sanity, Amanda checks to see if the back passenger door is unlocked. She doesn't want to have to get the keys out if she doesn't have to.

Luckily, it opens right up.

"What are you doing?" Jeff asks her as Amanda helps him out of the way so that the car door doesn't hit him as she opens it.

"You have to hide in here, Jeff."

"What?"

"Like you said, he's going to come back out here looking for us. He won't expect you in here."

"But he'll see the keys are gone."

"Not if I put them back where they were."

"You're going back in there?!"

"We need his keys. And he's got Brittany."

"Are you fucking insane? He'll kill you."

"Not if I kill him."

"Amanda, this is crazy."

"What other choice do we have, Jeff? Tell me what other choice we have." A lump is building up in her throat again, but she pushes back the tears. She can't break down. She has to keep it together.

"Now, come on," she tells him. "Let's get you in the car." She walks him closer so that he can lean into the backseat and she can reach in to turn off the courtesy light. Once she's flicked the light off, she helps push him in by lifting his legs for him. It's not close to as excruciating as getting him up the steps was. It's a relief how much easier it is.

"Here, take my cardigan," she tells him once he is settled into the backseat. She imagines that he must be cold with the blood loss. Not to mention that it's fairly cold outside to begin with.

"Thank you," he says as she takes it off and hands it over to him. She feels bad, because the right half of it is stained with his blood. But it's better than nothing.

"We're going to be okay," she tries to reassure him.

"You don't know that."

He's right. She doesn't know that they're going to be okay. And not knowing what else she can say or do for him, she quietly shuts the car door.

She stands looking at the house in front of her, the house she has to go back into. In the course of less than four hours, this house has gone from being a safe haven to being a place of hell. This was supposed to be a great time for all of them, a nice, relaxing break from their day-to-day lives.

But all of that has gone to shit now.

Heading back toward the house, she is overcome with dread, knowing that in an attempt to keep herself and her friends alive, she could very well be walking to her death.

chapter 17

The possibility that Amanda headed back to the house is confirmed for Russell as he sees that the back door to the basement is both shut and, as he notes as he pulls the handle, locked. He knows, what with his cutting the phone line and slashing the tires to their cars, that she couldn't have done anything further to prevent him from accomplishing exactly what it is he's set out to accomplish. She'll give up eventually. And then he'll shoot the bitch dead and there will be no more trouble.

He doesn't bother trying to break the lock. It's a sliding door, and he's got a hundred-something-pound unconscious body in the crook of his right arm. He backs away a little and, using his boot, kicks the glass as near the door handle as he can kick. Nothing happens. Frustrated, he kicks a second time. This time, he can feel that the glass is weakening. The third time does the trick. The shards fall mostly inside onto the carpet, but some make it outside into the grass directly in front of where he stands.

Adjusting his hold on Brittany, he bends over a little,

reaching through the hole that he has proudly made, and unlocks the door. He pulls his hand out from inside and slides the door open, dragging Brittany inside with him.

The first thing he notices, as he passes the pool table, is Kyle's body still lying where he left it. He's definitely dead.

And how about that other guy? Jeff, was that his name? Russell turns toward the stairwell and sees, to his shock, that Jeff is gone. "Fuck!" he shouts. It enrages him to think that Jeff is still alive, hiding somewhere. What a mess this has become, all thanks to his inability to prevent Amanda from fighting him off. He shouldn't have put his gun down on the bed so soon. He just wanted to strangle her, to make it a quiet death so that none of her friends down here in the basement would hear.

And as for Jeff, Russell should have shot him in the head like he did the other two. It would have guaranteed his death. But he was rushed, panicked over Amanda's escape.

He can't have gotten far, though. Either he is with Amanda or he is hiding somewhere on his own. But there is no way Amanda got him up those stairs, so that rules out the first possibility. He's got to be down in this basement somewhere, hiding. Well, it's time to find him and kill him for sure this time.

Exhausted from dragging Brittany, he drops her to the floor, beside her dead friend. As he pulls his pistol out of his coat pocket, he notices a light coming from in the room straight ahead. Could Jeff be in there?

He walks past the stereo system, and as he peers into the room, he sees static on the large screen straight ahead and rows of chairs facing the screen. It's a home theater, he realizes. This is a perfect place for a wounded person to hide. Jeff could have crawled into this room and hidden somewhere within all of the seats. The only thing is that there's no trail of blood leading inside. But maybe Jeff stopped bleeding, at least as profusely as he had to have been. It's worth looking.

HITTING THE FLOOR BRINGS BRITTANY back to consciousness— an unwelcome pain to her already aching body. As she opens her eyes, she realizes that she is back in the basement. How has she gotten here?

Oh, now she remembers. *Him.* She can feel the dried- up blood around her nose. She wonders if her nose has been broken. It hurts so much.

She picks her hand up off the floor to feel her nose. She wants an idea of how bad it is, although she is afraid to find out.

She knows for sure that it is bad as her fingers touch the bare bone sticking out of her skin. She must look like absolute hell.

She can hear footsteps and Russell's cursing coming from what sounds like the theater. She assumes he's looking for Amanda. Could she have gotten away, driven off to get help? She seriously hopes so.

But what if help doesn't come in time, if it's even coming at all? Russell is going to kill her. At least for now, he's distracted with trying to find Amanda. She should take advantage of his distraction and make a run for it. He's in the theater now. She can run up the steps and drive off to get help, even if Amanda has already done so. But she'll need to get her keys out of her bedroom first. That will pose a problem if Russell notices that she's gotten away, which he most likely will in no time. If worse comes to worst, she can just lock herself up in her bedroom and call 9-1-1. Or she could go into one of the other bedrooms up there. Whichever has a landline.

One thing she knows for certain is that she needs to get out of this basement, where she is completely vulnerable to Russell.

But first, she needs to get up off of this floor. And this is going to be anything but an easy feat, considering the pain she is in.

AMANDA CAUTIOUSLY STEPS INSIDE THE house, not bothering to shut the front door behind her and run the risk of being heard. And besides, it might make Russell think she's outside instead of here in the house.

She made sure to check the sidelights before coming into the house. She wasn't about to just step inside and have Russell here waiting to kill her. But still, he could come right up those basement steps and find her standing here in the front hallway. She expects this to be the case at any moment, which is why she needs to think fast.

She sets the keys down on the front table. While Russell may suspect that she and Jeff are outside with the front door being open, she hopes that the keys being here will make the Jeep the last place for him to look for them. This logic had better fool him, because she doesn't have much else to bank on while looking for a way to kill him or at least knock him out so she can get his keys.

She is startled as she hears shouting from what sounds to be down in the basement. It's Russell's voice. He just shouted, "Where the fuck is he?"

He must be looking for Jeff. Wow. So they really have fooled him, and unintentionally so. With the back door to the basement locked, she never thought Russell would have suspected anything other than the fact that she dragged Jeff up the stairs with her. But she is happy to be wrong.

She quietly heads down the hallway and toward the kitchen so she can hear what's going on down in the basement a little better. She fears that Russell will come up the stairs at any moment after realizing that Jeff isn't down there. She wonders how long he's been looking, if he's scouted out the whole basement already.

As she steps into the kitchen, she realizes that it isn't good being empty-handed, with no form of defense. She needs a weapon. She wonders if Jennifer's parents have a gun in the house. Could it be up in one of the bedrooms? She doesn't want to go back up there, though, and see the bodies again. She doesn't even want to think about her dead friends because it only reminds her how vulnerable to Russell she truly is. And she can't feel vulnerable right now. She needs to feel powerful, more so than the person who would have no trouble ending her life in the flash of a second.

She can't waste any time thinking about a gun that might not even be here in the first place. She's relieved to still hear Russell's shouting and cursing in the basement, but it's only a matter of time before he will come up here looking for her and Jeff. And she needs to be ready when he does.

She looks around the kitchen for something she can use against him. How about a knife? She directs her attention at the knife holder on the counter adjacent to the sink. It seems like the only solution aside from a gun.

But what about a baseball bat or something she's a little

more secure with using, something she knows for sure will do him in? Well, she isn't going to find a baseball bat in the kitchen. She's got to look elsewhere.

She is scared out of her mind. She could just leave now, make a run for it to the nearest residence, save herself. Or if she's lucky, there might even be a car on the road she can wave down. The chances of that are slim, though, given how late it is and the fact that they are in the middle of nowhere.

She didn't want to consider this option at first, not in front of Jeff. She knows that she could never forgive herself for leaving her friends to die. But it would still be so much easier, so much less of a risk. Because if she dies trying to get Russell's keys and to save Brittany in the process, assuming she is still even alive, then they all will die. At least this way, she knows she will get out of this. It will be a long time before Russell guesses she's made a run for it on the road, a long time of him looking for her in the house and again in the surrounding woods. And maybe Jeff will be able to get out of this, too, if Russell doesn't find him and if he can stay alive while waiting.

As for Brittany, she will be on her own. If she isn't dead already, she probably will be by the time help arrives.

BRITTANY TURNS HER HEAD AS little as possible to see if Russell has made it to the room furthest into the basement, which looked and sounded to be where he was headed as he passed her. She was about to get up and try to make a run for it a few moments ago, but then Russell came out of the theater once he'd come to the realization that the "he" he is looking for wasn't in there. Does he mean Kyle, Jeff, Nick? Who is he referring to?

She can't see past the pool table. She's got to turn her head a little more to see into the back room. As she does so, she sees, out of the corner of her eye, Kyle's feet next to hers. She lifts her head up a little to get a better look.

She sees the rest of Kyle's lifeless body lying beside hers. She can't bear to look at him. It's too painful.

Looking past Kyle's body, she sees that the door is open. She can hear Russell cursing in there.

Never having set foot in the room herself, she has no idea how big or small it is. But she knows that at any moment, Russell will be out of there if he doesn't find who he is looking for. And then what? She doesn't want to stick around to find out.

She turns her head in the opposite direction toward the stairwell to get a better idea of how fast she could get to the steps and be out of range of being shot at by Russell. She knows she will have to be quick as lightning.

Just beside the bottom of the steps, she can see a large blood stain but no body. She realizes that that is where Jeff must have been.

So Jeff must be who Russell is looking for now. She hopes that he isn't down here still, hiding in one of the rooms. Because if he is, then Russell will kill him. That's a given.

Maybe he and Amanda found each other and they're *both* off getting help. She hopes so. Regardless of where Jeff is or what he is doing, she is comforted by the thought that he is probably still alive. She hopes to God that it stays that way.

She needs to get up off of this floor. There is no more time to waste.

Swallowing the pain, she forces herself up from the ground. The aching in her back and the pain in her nose are next to unbearable, but she does her best to keep her focus on the immediate, however dire of a physical condition she is in.

Once she is up, she checks her immediate surroundings for something she can use as a weapon in case she needs one. Not that it will do any good against a gun, but still.

She spots the almost empty bottle of rum on the coffee table. If worse comes to worst and she can't get to her keys in time, she can sneak up on Russell and hit him over the head with it—

"Where are you, fucker?!" Russell's voice is closer now than it was. She's got to make a run for it. He's going to come out of that room any second now and see her standing here. She can't let that happen.

She worries that there isn't time to make it to the stairs. He'll see her and shoot at her. What about the theater? She could hide in there. It's the closest room to the stairs.

There's no more time to decide. In a panic, she picks up the bottle of liquor and runs into the theater, hoping to God she hasn't been seen.

As he steps out of the boiler room, Russell sees that Brittany has disappeared. Has she gone and run upstairs? It's no worry to him. She'll be in for the same surprise as her friends. No phone. No car. What's a girl to do but be killed?

He looks over at the closed door on his right, the only room in which he hasn't searched for Jeff. She could have gone in there. He doubts it, though. She had a chance to run for it. Why would she have done anything other than that?

Still, though, Jeff could be in there.

He steps over Kyle's body and opens the door. As he peers

inside, through the dark of what he sees to be a bathroom, he doesn't see either of them. But the shower is straight ahead and the curtain is drawn. Jeff could very well be in the bathtub. It's the only place left to look for him. This has to be the place then.

Stepping into the bathroom, he walks to the shower and pushes the curtain to the side.

No one is in the bathtub. No one is in this bathroom. The most shocking thing about this discovery is not the discovery itself but the fact that it tells Russell that Jeff is not in this basement. And as for Brittany, well, she probably isn't either.

Walking out of the bathroom, he steps over Kyle's body again, satisfied for the moment over the fact that he was able to kill at least some of them right off the bat. But as for the other three, well, they are some tough little fuckers. He'll give them that. To think that Amanda got Jeff all the way up those steps. He wonders if *he* could even do that. And then Brittany. Will this girl ever give up?

Not until he kills her.

She could have gone into the theater. It's a possibility. He ought to check there first before he goes upstairs. "Oh, Brittany?" he calls out to her. "Where did you go, Brittany?" He heads past the stereo system once again. "You can't hide from me forever, you know."

BRITTANY STANDS AGAINST THE WALL next to the theater's entrance, frustrated with herself for not having just made a run for it. She heard Russell opening the bathroom door. It was her chance. But she knew he would be out of there in no time.

And then he came out. And it was too late.

She is terrified that Russell will come in here and find her. She is glad to have the bottle in her hand, although she isn't the least bit ready to fight him again. It didn't work out the past two times; what makes her think she'll be any more successful now?

His voice and footsteps are coming closer. She prays that he will pass this room and check upstairs instead. In seconds, she'll know.

Her whole body tenses as she hears his footsteps right outside the entrance, just feet away from where she stands. He is going to come in here and check. She knows it. The anticipation puts knots in her stomach, knots so tight that she feels like she is going to explode and ruin any chances she has of defending herself and ultimately surviving.

RUSSELL WILL BE SURE TO kill Brittany as soon as he finds her. He wishes he could save her for last just for the sheer fun of it, but she is adding too much of a mess to what has already become a disaster.

He searched for Jeff inside all the rows of seats. He'll do the same for Brittany. She probably isn't in there. What good would it do her? She wouldn't be able to get to a dead phone or to her useless car.

But he'll check anyway. He can't be too sure of anything after tonight's turn of events.

As he steps into the theater, he instantly sees her out of the corner of his eye.

And then he feels the pain of being hit over the head with the bottle before she drops the bottle to the floor and runs out of the theater, away from him.

The pain is unbelievable. Russell feels the pressure to his head and the intense ringing in his ears that comes with that pressure. It's like nothing he's ever felt before. He never knew being hit over the head with a glass bottle could be so excruciating. It's everything he can do to stand up straight and maintain his focus.

He can't help but taste the wetness saturating his face. He knows it's blood. *His* blood. She got him good this time.

The rage is what comes next. Russell begins to seethe with anger, more anger than he has had all night. More anger than he had when he found out she was looking for him. More anger than he has had in his entire life.

"Oh, you fucking cunt," he says, gripping his pistol firmly. "I'm going to fucking kill you."

He darts out of the theater after her with an animalistic determination brought on by his rage. This is going to be the best kill he has ever had. Better than killing her friends, her neighbor, her mother. She has unleashed the madman within him. Any inhibitions he had are gone now, obliterated.

He is relieved to see that she hasn't made it to the top set of steps. But she's about to make the turn. He isn't going to let that happen.

He aims his pistol at her and fires, hitting her in the back of her leg. He is gratified upon hearing her scream out in pain as she falls to the steps in agony, the blood spurting out of her leg like a fountain. *The bitch thought she could win, did she? Oh, well now, she's about to lose worse than she could ever have imagined.*

Sliding his gun into his coat pocket, he sees that he's got her good. This time she won't be recovering.

Walking over to the stairs, he grabs her by both of her legs, dragging her back down. "Help me!" she screams in protest. "Help me!"

But he knows that help isn't going to come for her. Even if her friends have gone for help, he will have killed her by the time it arrives. And if anyone happens to be upstairs, after hearing the gunshot, they will be far too terrified to come down and help her. He knows it's over for her now. He can finally put an end to this mess.

Once he has her back down at the bottom of the steps, he forces her up by the hair and throws her into the wall across from the bar. He is ready to act on the urges he has suppressed for so long. It is time to let the animal in him take over.

Wrapping his hands around her neck, he begins to choke the life out of her. She gasps and gags, desperate for air. But he has no intention of showing her any mercy. His hands couldn't be wrapped around her neck any harder than they are now.

"You're going to die now," he whispers to her. It pleases him to see her fighting for the air she can't have. It's what she gets for prying into business she should have left alone. She thought she could have him put away? Well, she was dead wrong.

Brittany can see through Russell's wide-open eyes that he is getting a perverse pleasure out of strangling her like this. Although she has accepted death, there is still a part of her craving life. But she is far too weak to try to push him off of her or to fight him off in any other way. All she can do is take in his words and accept that this is how she is going to die. How stupid of her to think that she could escape this man. He's wanted to kill her, and he's now doing just that.

And to think she brought this on herself by searching him out and trying to bring him to justice like she did. If she just left the past in the past, none of this would be happening right now.

These are Brittany's last thoughts as consciousness slips away yet again, only this time not to return. Death is very near. She can feel it.

The job is almost done. Russell knows that Brittany doesn't have much longer to live the way he has his hands around her neck. But despite her obvious drifting away into the unknown, he has no intention of loosening his grip. Not until she is dead and the uninhibited animal in him is fully satisfied—

He suddenly feels a sharp pain in his back that hurts like hell. It takes him a second to realize what has happened: he has been stabbed.

Succumbing to the pain, Russell lets go of Brittany's neck, allowing her body to fall to the floor.

Brittany feels light as a feather as she slides down against the wall. As she begins to gasp for air, the lightheadedness overtakes her for a few seconds, depriving her of the ability for anything.

Once the lightheadedness passes and the world around her comes back into focus, she notices the handle of Russell's gun sticking out of his coat pocket.

Is this really happening? she wonders in disbelief. Is she really still alive? How?

She decides not to question the circumstances for the moment. She directs her focus on the gun. She knows what she needs to do now. She can finally end this, once and for all.

She is startled as Russell falls to his knees. She realizes, however, that Russell has no intention of causing her harm when she sees the knife sticking out of his back and Amanda standing back by the stairs, looking terrified of the possible consequences of what she has just done.

She crawls away from Russell a bit before reaching into his pocket for his gun. Something about reaching for the gun makes her feel triumphant, like there is a higher power working to bring her justice since the world has failed to do so.

Once she's grabbed hold of the gun, she backs away from Russell a safe distance and allows herself to fall back down to the floor in relief. She looks over and sees that Amanda, who is still frozen in her spot by the stairs, is staring over at her with a hopeful urgency in her eyes as she realizes what Brittany is about to do.

Seeing that he is still kneeling on the floor in agony, she aims the pistol at his head. Her hand shakes as she does so. However, it isn't because she is nervous. It is because she is overcome with emotion at how this has all worked out. It is finally time for him to be at her mercy.

It doesn't bother her in the least to see him on his knees, crying out in pain. She has no pity for this man who murdered her mother and now one of her best friends. And how can she possibly forget the pain he has senselessly inflicted on her throughout the night?

"Please," she hears him begging. "Please, no." It's good to know that he doesn't want to die. It will make killing this son of a bitch all the more gratifying.

Without another moment's hesitation, she pulls the trigger.

She hears Amanda's screaming and sees her falling to the floor in a shaken fit as blood splatters the wall behind Russell's head. She sees her wrap her arms around her legs in fright as Russell's body falls toward Brittany to the floor.

Brittany stares at the gun as she sets it back down on the floor. Her hand still shakes. She is numb from it all but relieved nonetheless. Russell Thompson is dead.

chapter 18

Once Jeff is out of the Jeep and Amanda has his arm wrapped around her so he won't fall, Brittany begins limping down the driveway to Russell's car. Every step she takes allows the pain to sear through her body. Between her leg and her nose, she doesn't know which is worse. They both feel like hell.

As she peers down at her leg, she sees that the blood is beginning to come through the second rag. When she and Amanda got up to the kitchen, she was able to tie two dishrags around her leg to help stop the bleeding. But the rags aren't proving to be much of a tourniquet.

She reaches into her pants pocket and pulls out Russell's keys. She doesn't want to be touching his keys. She surely doesn't want to be riding in his car. She doesn't want anything to do with this man. She wants him out of her life. But she knows that he'll always be in her memories, haunting her until the day she dies. It's her cross to bear.

She looks behind her to see if Amanda is doing okay with Jeff. She doesn't look comfortable, but she's managing.

Brittany offered to help carry Jeff, but Amanda won't let her because of her leg.

She is amazed by Amanda. Who would have known she had it in her to carry her wounded friend up a flight of stairs to get him somewhere safe, only then to come back for her other friend? She saved their lives. They'd be dead if it wasn't for her.

Brittany presses the unlock button on the remote. When she doesn't hear a clicking sound, she pulls on the latch to the back passenger door and it opens. She makes sure to open it up all the way. Amanda will need room to get Jeff into the backseat.

As she peers in, she is glad to see that there isn't anything on the backseat for her to have to clear off. She is beyond exhausted, beyond emotionally drained. She doesn't know how she is going to get through it this time. She is afraid that she will never feel safe again, that she will never get out of the state of horrified despair that she is in now. She doesn't even know if she is happy to be alive right now. Maybe it would have been better if Russell killed her. At least that way, she would be at peace.

But she's got her friends to think of, Amanda especially. Amanda came back for her. Amanda risked getting killed and came back for Brittany to save her life. To think that she is blessed to have such a person in her life, well, that is reason enough for Brittany to go on.

Stepping away from the back door to the car, Brittany sees that the trunk is open.

As Amanda and Jeff reach the car, she moves out of their way and limps over to the trunk to shut it.

As she is about to shut the trunk, she stops herself for a

moment as she catches a glimpse of what is inside. Among the empty plastic bags and the jump-start cables are two tanks of gasoline.

Nothing can surprise her at this point; she is already in such shock. But this is not something she expected. She did not expect that Russell was planning to burn the place down once he'd killed them all. The sick fuck was planning to burn them all to ashes to try to cover up the evidence that it had been murder.

Too bad it didn't work out for him. She'd like to burn *him* to ashes and watch his body disintegrate in the flames. It seems as though it isn't enough just to have killed him the way she did, not after all he'd done to her, her friends, and her family. Not after all that he has taken from her. She wishes it could have been a slower, more painful death like he tried to make hers.

But it's over now. All she can do now is move on and be thankful that she and two of her friends have made it out alive. And be thankful that Russell hasn't.

"You ready?"

Brittany is forced from her thoughts as Amanda tells her it's time to go. She quickly checks to make sure the lids to both gasoline tanks are on tight. She could just take them out of the trunk and leave them on the driveway, but she doesn't want Amanda to see. No more upset tonight. She's already brought enough hell on her friends.

She closes the trunk tightly and hands the keys over to Amanda.

Amanda takes the keys from her as she shuts the door to the backseat. Brittany is pretty confident that Jeff is going to be okay despite the amount of blood he has lost. She doesn't know how soon it will be until he is in an ambulance or at a hospital, but he needs medical attention desperately. And so does Brittany. It must be frightening for Amanda to look at her. She's surprised she can even breathe right with the bone sticking out of her nose like it is.

"Brittany," Amanda says to her once she has circled the front of the car to get to the driver's door. Brittany, who is about to slide into the passenger's seat, looks over at Amanda across the roof of the car.

"It was *him*, wasn't it?"

Brittany knows exactly what Amanda means by this. Looking away from her friend in shame, shame over the fact that this whole thing has been her fault, she nods her head.

Once Brittany and her friends are settled into the car, the car of the man who tried to kill them, the car of Russell Thompson, Amanda starts the engine and turns on the heat so that Jeff won't be so cold in the back.

As they drive off into the night, Brittany acknowledges the fact that she and her friends are both leaving behind and bringing with them a tragedy. It is a tragedy that started with just Brittany and her mother over a half a decade ago. But now, the tragedy has extended itself, given itself a second part. A tragedy of a young woman seeking justice for her mother and the man who stopped at nothing to cover up his past wrongdoings.

And yet again, she has survived the tragedy. Her tragedy. And this time, she has put an end to it, once and for all.

The tragedy of Brittany Taylor.

Eric Burns is currently an undergraduate student at Saint Mary's College of Maryland. He is from Baltimore, Maryland; this is his first book.